DESERT ISLAND DUKE

A RUTHLESS RIVALS NOVELLA

KATE BATEMAN

Desert Island Duke is a work of fiction. Names, places, and incidents either are products of the author's imagination or are used fictitiously. Any resemblance to actual events, locales, or persons, living or dead, is entirely coincidental.

Copyright © 2022 by Kate Bateman

All rights reserved.

No part of this book may be reproduced in any form or by any electronic or mechanical means, including information storage and retrieval systems, without written permission from the author, except for the use of brief quotations in a book review.

Digital ISBN: 979-8-9873291-3-9

Print ISBN: 979-8-9873291-4-6

Cover design © by The Swoonies 2022.

❀ Created with Vellum

CHAPTER 1

*L*ady Caroline Montgomery glared at the body farther down the beach and let out a snort of aggravation. Five minutes ago, she'd thought being shipwrecked alone on a tropical island was the worst thing that could have happened to her.

She'd been wrong. So wrong.

Being shipwrecked *alone* would have been delightful—in comparison. She was clever, resourceful, and accustomed to challenging situations such as this. Alone, she would have been fine.

Fate, however, hadn't granted her that small mercy. Not content with sending a typhoon to wreck the *Artemis* and separate her from her beloved family, the cruel universe had saddled her with *him*.

Maximillian Cavendish.

His Grace, the fourteenth Duke of Hayworth.

The most infuriating man on seven continents and the very last creature Caro would have chosen as a fellow survivor— including the *Artemis's* pig, which she'd affectionately named The Duke of Pork.

Hayworth lay on his side, his face turned away from her, but there was no mistaking his dark, tousled hair or those improbably broad shoulders. For such an indolent scoundrel, he had a remarkably healthy physique.

Caro stomped toward him along the sand, her damp skirts hampering her strides, and tried to squash the tiny kernel of panic at the stillness of his giant frame.

"You'd better not be dead," she panted crossly.

He didn't move when her shadow fell across his face, so she prodded him, none too gently, with the toe of her boot. "Hayworth? Are you dead?"

He wasn't. She could see his shoulder rising and falling as he breathed, and a knot of something she refused to label as relief loosened inside her. She told herself it was because she didn't want to be saddled with a corpse.

Still, he seemed to be unconscious. Considering how obnoxious the man was when awake, she would have preferred to leave him that way, but Caro supposed she had a moral obligation to rouse him. She poked him again in the ribs.

He let out a low groan, but his eyes remained closed.

Caro dropped to her knees beside him, grasped his shoulder, and gave him a hard shake. The muscles beneath the wet material of his jacket were incredibly solid.

She tried not to notice.

"Wake up, you insufferable oaf! It's too hot to dig you a grave."

She gave him another push, then almost jumped out of her skin when he sucked in a gasping breath and began coughing uncontrollably.

Caro gave him a few helpful whacks between his shoulder blades.

He flailed his arm and shoved her away. "Hoi! Stop that! I'm not dead, damn you!"

His voice was rough and raspy and she cursed the little frisson the sound always produced in her stomach. She scuttled backward like a crab as he rolled over onto his back and took a great lungful of air that made his chest expand even more.

He slung his forearm over his forehead, shielding his eyes from the blinding sun, and squinted up at her with a frown.

His eyes were an extraordinary turquoise, the same blue as the lagoon before them. Caro narrowed her own eyes in irritation. It was a stupid color for a man. Truly. It should have made him look pretty and vapid, like a doll, but instead they'd been paired with black-as-night eyebrows, a straight slash of a nose, and cheekbones that could have hewn granite. The effect was aggravatingly attractive.

His chin was covered in a peppering of dark stubble, as fine-grained as the white sand that stuck to his cheek, and Caro caught herself wondering what it would feel like against her palm.

Dear God, she must have sunstroke.

Hayworth, thankfully, was unaware of her ludicrous thoughts. He pushed himself into a sitting position with a groan and rested his head on his bent knees.

Caro scowled. She, no doubt, looked like a drowned rat. *He* somehow managed to look perfectly delicious, in a rumpled, careless, piratical sort of way. How had such an underserving wretch been endowed with such extraordinary good looks? It wasn't fair.

Maximillian Cavendish hadn't just been born with a silver spoon in his mouth – he'd been gifted the entire silver dinner service, too. Ever since his father's death, when Max had been a boy of merely nine, he'd been heir-apparent to his childless uncle, the thirteenth Duke.

Caro had made his acquaintance years ago; he was one of her brother William's closest friends, and she could unwaveringly state that Hayworth had displayed a confidence that bordered on arrogance even *before* his uncle's demise had promoted him from duke-in-waiting to *His Grace* last year.

He was one of those people for whom everything seemed to come easily. In addition to sinful good looks, he possessed a fierce intelligence, a quick wit, and considerable charm—not that he'd ever wasted those last two attributes on her. He was irritatingly good at everything he tried; whether it was fencing, riding, or gaming at his club.

And, it seemed, surviving a shipwreck at sea.

He turned his head and caught her eye, and Caro's heart gave an uncomfortable little thump. She'd always both craved and hated his regard.

"You're right. I'm definitely not dead," he said. "If I was dead, you'd be naked."

CHAPTER 2

Caro's mouth fell open in shock. "I beg your pardon?"

"If I was dead," Hayworth repeated, his voice a deliciously low rasp from the salt water he'd ingested, "and in heaven, then the beautiful woman who greeted me would most definitely be naked."

Caro blinked. Beautiful? Had Maximillian Cavendish just called her *beautiful*?

She glanced around at the sky, the white sand, the palm trees swaying on the shore. What bizarre alternate universe was this? Was she *dreaming*? It was the only logical explanation. She pinched herself on the thigh, to make sure.

Nothing happened.

Hayworth didn't seem to notice her confusion.

"Then again," he used one hand to ruffle the sand from his tousled hair, "I might be dead and in hell. That's very possible. In which case, being greeted by a fully-clothed siren who *looks* like she should be naked, but never takes her clothes off, well, that would be the very definition of punishment, wouldn't it?"

Caro assumed that was a rhetorical question.

"You're delirious," she said stoutly. "Did the lifeboat hit you on the head when it overturned?"

He rubbed his scalp again, as if searching for lumps. "Don't think so."

"Look at me."

He glanced at her again, and she stared deeply into his eyes, searching for any sign of recognition. Or, indeed, sanity.

He stared back at her solemnly. And then his mouth curved into a slow, wicked, openly appraising smile that made her stomach swirl dangerously. His gaze dropped to her lips, as if he was thinking of kissing her.

What on earth was happening?

"Stop being ridiculous," she scolded. "I'm not an angel or a devil. You know who I am. I'm Caroline. Caro Montgomery. William's sister."

"Caro." He repeated the name with a kind of wonder, rolling it around his mouth as though saying it for the first time. "Hello Caro. I'm glad you're not dead."

"As am I," she muttered uncertainly.

Maybe that was it. Maybe *she* was the one who was dead, and in some dreadful underworld where her only companion was the one man guaranteed to drive her mad for all eternity. It made a horrible kind of sense. He'd cursed her when she was alive. It stood to reason that he'd haunt her when she was dead, with his irresistible smirk and his perfect, unattainable body.

He reached out and smoothed a strand of salt-encrusted hair back from her forehead. His palm stroked her cheek, and Caro froze in surprise at the appreciative look on his face.

What was *wrong* with him? He'd never looked at her in such a way before. He usually regarded her with a mocking expression that suggested she was the amusing, unwitting, butt of his jokes. Did he *really* not recognize her?

"So, we've established that you're Caro," he murmured.

"Which would make me . . ?" He let the sentence trail off in a questioning uplift of sound.

"Cavendish," Caro said irritably. The idiot was clearly fooling with her, pretending he'd forgotten his own name.

"Huh," he said, sounding surprised. "Do people call me Cav?"

She was getting more exasperated by the second. "No, they don't. Cavendish isn't your first name. It's your family name, you dolt. Your Christian name is Max."

"Short for Maximillian, I assume?"

She batted his hand away. "Yes. Stop pretending you don't remember."

He let out a short laugh. "You think I'm *feigning amnesia*?"

"Of course you are. It's precisely the kind of thing you'd do. Teasing me is one of your favorite pastimes."

His lips twitched again. "It is? Teasing you?"

"Yes," she gritted out. "You've been mocking me and laughing at me from the first moment we met." That was absolutely true.

"And when was that?" he prompted.

"Years ago. You used to come and visit Will during the school holidays. And since then, every time we were in London, whenever my family was between expeditions."

"Expeditions?"

"My father's one of England's best-known butterfly experts. We travel all around the world looking for them."

"Hmm." His reply was non-committal, and she studied him again, more closely.

"Do you really not remember?"

"I remember your face," he said vaguely, "But as to the rest—" he gave a shrug that lifted his broad shoulders.

Caro was still suspicious. How could he remember her, but not his own name? It was extremely unlikely. Then again, the odds of them both surviving a shipwreck and being washed up, alive, on this same stretch of sand were infinitesimally small too. Perhaps he *was* telling the truth.

"Do you remember being a soldier? You served with Will at Waterloo."

His brow furrowed again. "Yes, I do remember that. My horse was shot out from under me."

Caro bit her lip. She'd heard the same thing from her brother's account of the battle. It was yet another example of Hayworth's charmed life that he'd emerged from that infamous bloodbath with hardly a scratch.

"Do you remember anything else about yourself?" Surely the man would recall he was a *duke,* for heaven's sake.

He paused, as if racking his brains. "I know I like peppermint."

Caro almost threw her hands up. This simply couldn't be true.

And then the most wicked thought bubbled up in her brain. Perhaps he really *didn't* remember. Perhaps fate was giving her this tiny sliver of opportunity to bring the arrogant devil down a peg or two. To level the playing field between them.

On this island, he wouldn't be the smug, superior friend of her brother, the high-and-mighty Duke of Hayworth. And she wouldn't be his best friend's little sister. They could start again, as equals. As simply Caro and Max. A man and a woman. Two people stuck on an island, working together.

It was an extremely alluring thought.

He was still staring at her in that strange, slightly besotted way, and Caro schooled her face into a bland expression.

"It's good that you remember your time in the army." She patted him consolingly on the arm. "Do you remember what you did after that?"

She waited for him to shake his head, then sent him a wide smile. The kind of bright, reassuring smile she used to cheer up children when they'd scraped their knees or been bitten by an ant. "After you left the army you discovered your uncle—you're his heir, by the way—had left you nothing but an enormous pile of debt."

Caro had to bite her lip to stop herself from laughing at this monstrous falsehood. His uncle had indeed left him an enormous pile—of *money*—and a lovely country estate named Gatcombe Park which boasted no fewer than twenty-three bedrooms and a ballroom big enough to play cricket in.

Oh, she would roast in hell for this, but it was worth it. Even if she was greeted at the fiery gates by a fully-clothed Maximillian Cavendish who teased her for eternity with the possibility of seeing him naked, it would be worth it.

"My uncle?" Hayworth repeated slowly. "A mountain of debt. Are you sure?"

"Oh yes, very sure. William felt so sorry for you, having fallen on such hard times, that he offered you a job."

Now Hayworth was delightfully confused, and Caro couldn't resist giving him the *piece de resistance*. She cast around for a suitably lowering position.

"You're a groom at our house in Lincolnshire. William says you're wonderful with the horses."

The incredulous look on Hayworth's face—as if the very idea of being a groom offended him to the core—made Caro's heart pound with the certainty that he'd recognize the lie and call her out.

Instead, he squinted up at the sun. "If I'm a groom, what am I doing here?"

"You're doubling up as Will's valet," Caro temporized quickly. "His usual man, Timms, got sick the week before we were due to sail for Madagascar, so you came along instead."

She waited for him to explode in outrage at her perjury. In truth, he'd only been a passenger on the *Artemis* because he'd been returning from a visit to see his cousin in India.

Hayworth's lips did an odd little twitch, as if he was about to laugh, but then his expression sobered and he nodded. "Ah. A groomsman and sometime-valet. That makes sense. I *do* like horses. And I definitely remember how to tie a decent cravat."

His hand strayed to this throat, where his own bedraggled

neckcloth still hung incongruously about his neck. That it had survived the chaos of the pounding waves when they'd both been tossed from the lifeboat and thrust onto this sandy shore was another miracle.

He untied the sodden knot and tugged the thin strip of linen from his shoulders, revealing an intriguing wedge of tanned chest in the deep open V of his shirt.

Caro averted her eyes, but only after an indecently long look. When she glanced back up at him, guiltily, he'd turned his head away and was gazing out over the blue expanse of water in front of them.

"So. I'm Max and you're Caro," he said easily, and she was struck with the renewed suspicion that he was teasing her.

He squinted at the green shape of another island, visible on the near horizon. "How did we get here?"

CHAPTER 3

Caro couldn't quite believe that Hayworth was accepting her story so readily, but she swiveled around to face the water, too.

Playful waves tickled the white sand, and the surface of the water within the enclosure of the reef was as smooth as glass. Huge waves still crashed against the outer ring of coral, spending their force with a constant low rumble, but it was hard to reconcile this same scene with the furious, churning cauldron of wind and waves that had flung them both ashore the previous night. Apart from a few tangled piles of driftwood and other flotsam higher up on the beach, there was hardly a trace of the storm.

"The *Artemis* lost her topsail, then her rudder," Caro said evenly. "She was blown onto the rocks over there." She pointed westward. Another island could be seen in the distance, and the ship lay just offshore, lilting badly to one side. It had clearly sustained serious damage.

"When Captain Thomas gave the order to abandon ship, there was a great deal of confusion on deck. You and I somehow ended up in the same lifeboat. You tried to row us ashore, to that other island, but the waves kept pushing us this way. When we neared the reef, a huge wave overturned us; I remember rolling over and over in the water, certain I was about to drown, but I awoke this morning here, on the sand."

Caro shook her head in amazement. It all felt like a terrible dream.

Hayworth frowned. "So where are the rest of the passengers? Dear God, they didn't all drown? What of your family?"

Caro smiled at the bombardment of questions. He might have lost his memory, but his imperious, demanding ways were still intact.

"My family was in another lifeboat." She gestured toward the sliver of beach just visible across the strait. "They made it to shore, along with the rest of the passengers. Look, you can see them, moving about on the sand. I've counted them, and everyone seems to be there."

Hayworth gave a grunt. "Everyone except us."

"At least we're alive."

"What happened to our lifeboat?"

"I assume it must have smashed on the reef. I walked a little way up the beach, but I didn't see it."

Hayworth grunted again, then narrowed his eyes at the other island. It seemed tantalizingly close, but Caro knew that the distance was deceptive.

"It's too far to swim," he said, as if reading her thoughts. "Even if we held onto driftwood or made a raft. That's at least two miles, maybe three, and we already know there are hideously strong currents out there."

"And sharks." Caro added helpfully. "And probably jellyfish."

"Quite so." He slapped his hands on his thighs and stood, full of renewed purpose. "Seems we're stuck here until we're rescued, then."

"It shouldn't be long," Caro said, more to comfort herself than him. "They must have some undamaged lifeboats over there. They'll row over and save us."

"They *might*," Hayworth sounded skeptical. "But it would be extremely risky. A small rowboat could easily get swept out to sea and lost. It's more likely they'll see we're alive and decide not to chance it. If we can see them, they must be able to see us." He sent a jaunty wave toward the opposite beach.

Caro shielded her eyes and could just make out an answering wave from one of the little figures on the shore.

"If that's my father, I can guarantee he's got a spyglass trained on us right now."

Hayworth stretched his hand out to pull her up from the sand. "In that case, I'll be on my very best behavior."

Her stomach flipped as his large fingers enfolded hers, and she struggled gamely to her feet. He brushed a small avalanche of sand from his thighs and turned to survey the lush forest that ringed the perfect crescent of beach.

A series of tree-covered slopes rose steeply toward the center of the island, and Caro sent up a prayer of thanks that they weren't on a windswept, treeless speck of land no bigger than a handkerchief.

"Look at this place. It's paradise." He gestured at the foliage. "I see coconuts, and we can fish in the sea. All we need is a source of fresh water and some shelter, and we'll be able to survive here for weeks."

"*Weeks?*" Caro gaped. "We won't need to survive for weeks. People will come looking for us as soon as they realize the *Artemis* is overdue in Cape Town."

Hayworth raised his brows. "I bet we were blown off course. You said we were on our way from Madagascar?"

Caro nodded. "I heard Captain Thomas say we were being pushed north, towards the Seychelles."

"Well, there are hundreds of islands dotted about in these waters. Unless some local fisherman happens upon us, it really *could* take weeks for us to be found. We should hope for the best, but prepare for the worst."

"Dear God," Caro muttered, appalled. This wasn't Paradise; it was Purgatory.

Hayworth, however, seemed remarkably upbeat about the prospect of being stranded. Perhaps he really *had* taken a blow to the head. He strode purposely off across the beach, his long legs eating up the distance. "Come on, we need to get out of the sun."

Since there was nothing else to do, Caro followed him, trying not to notice the way his fawn breeches clung to his long legs.

As soon as they reached the shade of the coconut palms, he turned back to her. "Right. First things first. We need water, fire, and shelter."

"Agreed. This isn't the first time I've had to make camp, you know. I spent several months in the rainforests of Brazil, before we sailed to Madagascar."

Of course, in Brazil she'd had the support of her family and a small army of local helpers, but there was no way she'd admit that to Hayworth. She might not have much practical experience, but she was confident in her own resourcefulness.

"How fortunate, to have been stranded with someone so perfect," he said smoothly, and Caro narrowed her eyes, unsure whether he was being sarcastic or not.

"Between my time in the army," he continued, "and your experience of living in all sorts of exciting places, we should make an excellent team."

Caro gave an unconvinced sniff.

He spread his cravat over a nearby bush, then patted his sodden jacket. With a triumphant crow, he reached into a pocket and withdrew a brass object, about three inches long.

"Ha, look at this! A folding knife. Past Max was clearly a man of foresight."

"You don't remember putting it in your pocket?"

"No. But I *do* remember winning it from a rifleman in a game of cards in Portugal. It was just after Salamanca."

"You remember your time as a soldier, four years ago, but not what happened last week?" Caro couldn't keep the skepticism out of her voice.

Hayworth grinned. "I'm sure it'll all come back to me eventually."

Caro prayed that day came long *afte*r they'd both left this island. She was already regretting her impulsive fabrication. As soon as Hayworth remembered he was a duke, and not a groomsman, there would be hell to pay. He'd probably strangle her in fury—if this blasted island didn't finish her off first.

He coaxed the small silver blade from the handle with a practiced flick of his thumbnail and held it up for her inspection.

"Now, I know what you're thinking," he said, with a wicked smirk. "But size isn't everything. It's what you do with it that counts."

Caro's cheeks heated at his bawdy inference. She wasn't so innocent as to misunderstand his meaning. Men loved embarrassing women by alluding to the size of their manly accoutrements. Considering Hayworth's monumental confidence, she had little doubt that his own personal 'blade' was more than adequate. She made a concerted effort not to look down at the front of his breeches.

"It's not going to be much good for cutting down trees," she said briskly, "but it's better than nothing, I suppose."

"Exactly. This little blade might be the difference between life and death out here."

He placed it on a piece of driftwood, then stripped off his jacket and spread it on the bush next to his cravat. His still-damp shirt clung to him like a spurned lover, and when he tugged the bottom of it from the waistband of his breeches, Caro let out a strangled gasp.

"Wait! What are you doing?" Her voice had risen an octave in shock.

He paused with the hem of his shirt halfway up his torso.

"Taking my shirt off, of course. We need to dry out." He

gestured at her own wet clothing. "Come on. Off with 'em. This is no time to be missish."

Before Caro could argue, he'd whipped the shirt over his head to reveal a muscular chest that made her catch her breath.

Dear God, the man was indecently well-built. She'd always suspected it, thanks to the cut of his jackets and the snugness of his breeches, but having it confirmed so emphatically made her a little lightheaded.

He turned, completely at ease with being half-naked in front of her, and began draping the shirt over the bushes. Caro couldn't help staring at the incredible play of muscles rippling beneath his lightly tanned skin. He'd clearly spent time without his shirt in India. He was golden all over. Far more like a groomsman than a duke, in fact.

When his fingers dropped to the buttons of his falls, however, she put her hands on her hips in outrage. "You absolutely *cannot* remove your breeches!"

CHAPTER 4

*H*ayworth sent her an amused glance, and Caro had the distinct impression that he'd had no intention of removing his breeches at all—that he'd only done it to get a rise out of her.

"Oh, very well. I suppose we should try to preserve your modesty. Although considering where we are, it's rather pointless. The rules of polite society can't possibly be upheld in a place like this."

Caro frowned. He had a good point. And she was definitely still damp.

Her dress—a sheer, sprigged muslin that was the perfect weight to counter the oppressive heat of the tropics—was practically transparent when wet, as it was now. Mercifully, she was also wearing her favorite long cotton petticoat, a set of short stays, and a knee-length cotton chemise as the final layer against her skin.

When the order to abandon ship had come last night, she'd tugged her leather ankle boots over her stockings and thrown a thin woolen shawl around her shoulders before her father had bustled her out into the passageway and up onto the heaving deck.

Her shawl had been lost to the churning waves, and in hindsight it was lucky her skirts hadn't prevented her from swimming. The weightless fabric had billowed up in the water, like a jellyfish, allowing her to kick her legs. If she'd been wearing a thick woolen skirt, and multiple petticoats, she would probably have been dragged down to a watery grave.

Still, perhaps learning the contents of Davy Jones's locker would have been preferable to disrobing in front of Maximillian Cavendish right now.

"I'm not taking *anything* off," Caro said stubbornly. "Except for my boots." She bent to undo the laces.

Hayworth merely shrugged and, after kicking a driftwood log over and checking it for insects, sat down to remove his own boots. He gripped the heel of one and tugged, and when it slid free, a stream of water and sand poured out onto the ground.

He sighed, as if pained. "They'll never be the same now, you know."

Caro was about to retort with a sarcastic comment about how he could afford ten more pairs, then remembered he was supposed to be a penniless groomsman and closed her mouth.

Since her stockings were wet, she took them off too, and wriggled her toes in the pleasantly warm sand.

Hayworth did the same, and she shot a sneaky glance over at his bare feet, hoping they'd prove to be one part of his body that was ugly, but they were long and elegant, just like the rest of him.

"You really should take more off," he said.

His tone made it sound like a perfectly reasonable suggestion, instead of perfectly indecent.

"You can't be comfortable, and there's no point in suffering just for the sake of propriety. I hate to break it to you, Miss Montgomery, but whatever reputation you might have had before this disaster has long since evaporated."

He sounded annoyingly pleased at the prospect that she might be ruined.

"My reputation, or lack of it, is the least of my problems right now, *Mister* Cavendish."

Caro took a gleeful delight in omitting his honorific title. "I'm sure there are scores of young ladies back in London who'd choose death over dishonor, but I'm not one of them. I'm glad to be alive. If the *ton* considers me ruined because I've been marooned on an island with an unmarried gentleman—through absolutely no fault of my own—then there's very little I can do about it. Fortunately, I care far less about finding a husband than I do about finding something to eat and drink."

He grinned. "A woman of independence. I like that. But still, we can't have you catching a fever from lounging about in damp clothing. If there was one thing the army taught me, it was to always stay warm and dry."

Caro let out an exasperated groan. In truth, she *was* uncomfortable. The steel wires in her stays were pressing into her ribs, and every inch of her was covered in scratchy sand.

"Oh, *fine*."

Turning her back to him, she slipped out of her dress and stepped out of her petticoat. After a moment of indecision, comfort won out over modesty, and she unlaced the front of her stays, too. She slipped the garment from her shoulders with a sigh of relief, and draped it over a piece of driftwood in the sun.

Risking a glance over her shoulder, she found Hayworth shirtless in just his breeches, looking like a sun-kissed Robinson Crusoe. She, now in nothing but her knee-length cotton chemise, probably looked like an escapee from an asylum. Or a very bedraggled ghost.

The only way to get through this situation was obviously to ignore her embarrassment and concentrate on the task in hand, namely: survival.

"It's still early. We should walk up the beach and try to find fresh water. There's no point setting up a camp miles away from something drinkable."

Hayworth nodded. "Agreed. If we can't find a stream, then we'll have to bash open some coconuts. Or find a puddle of rainwater. We can leave our clothes here to dry."

The two of them set off, keeping to the shade of the trees that fringed the beach as much as possible. The sandy bay ended in a rocky headland, which they reached without finding any stream or even trickle of water running onto the beach.

"We have to see what's around these rocks. Hopefully it's another bay."

Caro glanced at her bare feet. "They look too sharp to climb over. We should wade around, if it's not too deep."

Hayworth ventured into the shallow water, keeping to the sandy spaces between the rocks, and Caro followed in his wake. The water was astonishingly clear, and shoals of colorful fishes raced around their legs.

"Watch out for sea urchins," she warned.

"I wish we had a fishing pole. Or even just a hook and line. I could catch us some dinner."

"You could make a spear out of a stick," she suggested. "That might work. Or we could try to catch some of those crabs."

Scores of the armored little creatures crowded the rocks, scuttling into hiding holes whenever they got near.

With a final clamber over some partly-submerged rocks, they rounded the headland and discovered another perfect crescent, this one a little smaller than the one they'd been on before. Caro's heart gave a jolt as she noticed a disrupted section of sand about a hundred yards away.

"Look! Is that a stream?"

Hayworth set off at a brisk jog, and Caro let him go, disgusted with his athleticism. It was far too hot to run.

"It could just be seawater!" she shouted after him.

Before she was even halfway there, he dropped to his knees

and lifted a handful of liquid to his mouth. His whoop of triumph made her quicken her pace, and as she neared, she saw a steady trickle of clear water flowing out from the forest and down to the water's edge.

"Is it drinkable?"

He splashed his face with a laugh of delight. "Yes. It's wonderful! Have some."

She crouched at his side and scooped a handful to her lips, so desperate for a drink she didn't even care about the leaves and sticks floating about in it. She closed her eyes on a groan of pleasure. "Oh, dear God, that's good."

She took another long drink, then splashed her face, glad to remove the sticky salt and sand from her skin. When she glanced at Hayworth, she blushed to find his gaze fixed on her wet lips.

He coughed, as if there was something in his throat, and looked quickly away, then busied himself with washing the back of his neck.

When he finally stood, it was to inspect the foliage around them. He indicated a little clearing set back from the beach, sheltered by the trees, beyond the line of debris left by the high tide.

"We should make camp here. It's stupid to try to carry water back around to the other beach."

"But we'll be out of sight of the other island. My family will think something terrible has happened to us if we disappear."

"We'll go back and wave twice a day, so they can see us."

Caro sighed, accepting defeat. "Fair enough. If you go back for our clothes, I'll gather some sticks and branches to make a shelter."

He nodded, and Caro watched him retreat. Realizing she was staring at the tempting curves of his buttocks outlined by his tight, damp breeches, she forced herself to look away and get to work.

CHAPTER 5

*A*s soon as he was sufficiently far away, Max allowed the laugh that had been brewing in his chest for the past hour erupt. He shook his head at the shameless tales Caro Montgomery had concocted.

Destitute groomsman, indeed!

Oh, she was a little minx.

When he'd first opened his eyes this morning and seen her angelic features surrounded by a blinding halo of sunlight, he'd experienced a brief, understandable, moment of confusion. Since he only awoke next to Caro Montgomery in his wildest, most wicked dreams, he'd assumed he was still asleep.

That delusion had disappeared almost immediately, but when Caro had started spouting her outrageous torrent of misinformation—presumably just for the perverse pleasure of bedeviling him—he'd been so entertained that he hadn't bothered to correct her.

It had ever been thus between them.

She'd been right to say that he loved to tease her. As a schoolboy, he'd looked forward to his visits to her family home with breathless anticipation, hiding his delight at sparring with her behind mock disapproval and counter-teasing that had developed into a dangerously thrilling flirtation.

Fantasies of kissing her, and more, had invaded his dreams for years.

As they'd grown older, and Caro had ventured out into society, he'd watched with increasing disapproval as other young men had begun to appreciate her sparkling eyes and irreverent wit. But despite lusting after her to an inordinate degree, she was still his best friend's sister—which meant she was not the girl for a quick tumble in the sheets, but rather the kind of girl one married.

Back then, Max had considered himself far too young to settle down, but he'd breathed a silent sigh of relief each time he'd heard she'd turned down another marriage proposal.

In his foolish immaturity, he'd been a classic dog-in-the manger; he hadn't been able to admit that he wanted her for himself, but he hadn't wanted anyone else to have her, either.

He shook his head at his own youthful stupidity.

Caro put him in mind of the butterflies her father was so fond of studying; effortlessly beautiful and yet elusive, flitting from one group of people to another, delighting all she encountered, but never settling in one place for too long. A transitory beauty as beguiling as a South American swallowtail.

He'd missed her whenever she'd accompanied her parents and twin sisters on their various specimen-hunting expeditions around the world.

When he'd defied society's expectations and joined the fight against Napoleon as a cavalryman alongside her brother William, he'd come to realize just how much she meant to him. His numerous brushes with death, culminating in the nightmare of Waterloo, had solidified his feelings. He loved Caroline Montgomery with every thump of his still-beating heart.

Unfortunately, his determination to court her in earnest had been stymied by the fact that she'd left for a six-month-long trip to Brazil not three weeks after he'd returned to England. They'd been like ships that passed in the night.

Since London was a miserable place without her in it, Max had headed to his country seat, Gatcombe Park, and busied himself with setting the affairs of the estate in order. His uncle, the thirteenth duke, had—contrary to Caro's assertions—left the tenants happy and the ducal coffers full, and Max had quickly grown restless.

To pass the time until Caro came home, he'd taken a long-overdue trip to see his cousin in India. When Will had written to him, mentioning that Caro and the rest of her family would be traveling to Madagascar, in the Indian Ocean, the following month, Max had decided the fates were finally smiling down upon him.

He'd hastily arranged his own passage to the island to intercept them, and secured a cabin on their return ship, the *Artemis*, with the delightful prospect of spending the journey back to England wooing Caro so thoroughly that she'd finally see him as her perfect match.

That, clearly, hadn't gone to plan, but Max found that he couldn't be annoyed at the situation they'd suddenly found themselves in.

Was there such a thing as wishing for something *too hard*? He'd wanted to be alone with Caro, after all. Perhaps destiny had concocted this unlikely state of affairs to grant him his heart's desire in the most emphatic, inescapable way possible.

Because now he had her, all to himself.

For days, if not for weeks.

It was either the very best, or the very *worst* thing that could possibly have happened to him.

Obviously, he would have preferred somewhere a little less life-threatening. To be snowed in together at a cozy coaching inn, for example. Or stranded at a house party in the Highlands. Somewhere with decent food and adequate facilities.

Here there was the possibility of real bodily harm. Either one of them could get sick, or injured. They could slowly starve to death.

Max shook his head again. No. No harm would come to Caro. He'd die before he'd ever let that happen.

His protective instincts had always been strong, perhaps from having lost his father at such a young age, and he'd cared for the men under his command in the army as if they'd been his own flesh and blood. He'd done as much as humanly possible to keep them all alive while on campaign, and he would do exactly the same for Caro, now.

Not that he didn't think she was perfectly capable of surviving out here on her own. Caro was one of the most competent people he knew, male or female; it was one of the many things he loved about her. Most women of his acquaintance would have been swooning about on the sand right now, bemoaning their fate. Caro merely looked disappointed at the size of his pocket knife.

Max let out another snort of amusement. She hadn't been disappointed by the sight of his chest, though. She hadn't been able to look away when he'd stripped off his shirt.

The knowledge buoyed his spirits immensely.

He'd done a better job of pretending not to notice *her* body, although it had been a Herculean task. When she'd removed her damp dress, petticoat, and stays, it had taken a great deal of fortitude not stare at the tantalizing outline of her body so barely concealed by her chemise. He'd wanted to gather in his arms and never let her go, but such a move would have been met with either astonishment or fury from Caro.

He would have to bide his time.

Realizing he'd reached their clothes, Max gathered them up and started back along the sand.

CHAPTER 6

Caro had gathered a decent pile of driftwood by the time Hayworth returned. He arranged their still-damp clothes over some nearby rocks, then approached her with a grin.

"I have another surprise. When I picked up my jacket, I discovered my pocket watch."

The metal case glinted as he held it up. "It appears to be solid gold." He sent her a sideways, questioning look. "Which is odd."

"Why is it odd?"

"Well, this must be worth a few hundred pounds, at least. If I'm so short of money, how come I haven't sold it, to pay off some of my debts?"

Caro cursed inwardly. Was he trying to catch her out in her lie? Or did he truly not remember his own lofty position?

"It has sentimental value," she said quickly, praying it was true. "It belonged to your father. You couldn't bear to sell it."

Her pulse pounded as he flipped open the case and peered at an inscription engraved on the underside of the lid. Please, God, it hadn't been a gift from a friend, or, worse still, a mistress. If it said *'To Max, from your darling Sally,'* or something equally damning, she would be in a whole world of trouble.

"H.E.C." he read.

Caro breathed a silent sigh of relief at her lucky guess. "That stands for Henry Edward Cavendish. Your father."

"Ah. Excellent." He snapped the cover shut. "Not that having a watch will be very useful here. It's not as though we'll be receiving any visitors." He suddenly slapped his open palm against the back of his neck. "Ugh. Something bit me!"

"We need to make a fire. Smoke will keep the insects away."

"True, but how? If you think I'm going to spend hours rubbing sticks together, you can think again. One of my lieutenants tried it once, in Spain, and all he got for his trouble was blistered palms and an aching back."

"You won't need to rub sticks together."

His lips gave an amused little curl. "You've got a tinderbox hidden under that delightful chemise, have you? A brace of pistols, perhaps?"

Caro tried not to flush at the reminder of her state of undress. "Sadly not, but we can make a fire with that." She pointed at the timepiece in his hand.

"How? The hands are steel, I grant you, but they're tiny, and we don't have a flint to strike against them."

"No, look." She held her hand out, and he passed her the watch. She flicked it open. "The glass is curved. We can use it like a prism, to focus the sun's rays onto some tinder."

Caro bit back a little smile. This was one practical skill she *had* learned in Brazil, even though she and the twins had only done it for fun, and not for necessity. They'd burned patterns into leaves and set fire to Louisa's straw bonnet with their father's magnifying glass.

She glanced upward. "Unfortunately, we don't have any sun." Despite the oppressive heat, the sky was overcast. "But as soon as those clouds disappear, we can try it."

Hayworth nodded. "Let's make a shelter, then. It's bound to rain at some point. We'll need to keep dry, and so will our tinder."

He glanced up at the trees. "I don't think we should build directly under a coconut palm. I've heard of people being killed by falling coconuts."

Caro wondered if he'd heard those tales from the cousin he'd been visiting in India, but held her tongue. Perhaps he really *didn't* remember that part of his life. It seemed odd, that he should remember some things, but not others, but she was certainly no expert on head injuries.

He picked up a palm frond and began to sweep the area clear of debris. "This is a good spot. The rocks will shelter us from the worst of the weather."

Caro bit her lip at the unexpected sight of him performing the task of a scullery maid. "Have you ever made a shelter? Did you use tents in the army?"

"Well, as an officer, I was generally billeted in a local farmhouse whenever possible, but I did spend a few nights under the stars." The muscles in his arms flexed as he gathered a few fallen branches from among the trees. "We can make these into a frame, and then cover them with palm fronds and leaves."

"How will we tie them together? I didn't see any rope washed up on the shore, sadly."

Caro was loath to suggest they start ripping up her petticoats to make ties. She had few enough layers as it was. "I'll go look for some vines. And some food."

Hayward sent her an easy smile that made her heart patter. "Thank you."

"You should start by making a platform, raised off the ground," Caro added. "That's what we did in Brazil. There are all manner of things crawling about. Snakes and spiders and centipedes and whatnot."

He gave a theatrical shudder. "Good point. Scorpions I can deal with, but I am *not* a fan of spiders. Nasty, leggy things."

Caro pulled her still-damp boots back on and left him snapping branches and gathering lengths of wood. She ventured up the beach, on the lookout for anything that might be useful.

A few years ago, she'd read Daniel Defoe's novel *Robinson Crusoe*. The author had given his fictional castaway a host of tools and other items for *his* adventure. Crusoe had scavenged all manner of things from his ship, from blades and carpenter's saws, to sailcloth sheets and yards of rope and twine.

She and Hayworth, in contrast, had a folding knife, a pocket watch, and the clothes they stood up in.

Caro let out another huff of irritation. The fates, clearly, wanted them to suffer. Would it be too much to send them a bit of canvas and a nice long length of rigging?

She scanned the beach and then the lagoon, praying for a miracle, but there was nothing to see but sand and sparkling waves.

Several coconuts had washed up on the shore, so she collected them into a little pile for her return trip, along with some empty scallop-type shells. Then she ventured inland, careful to note her path by snapping twigs so she didn't get lost.

The foliage was much like the jungles she'd encountered in Brazil, a riot of green, but there were scores of plants she didn't recognize. Brightly-colored birds called to one another in the trees and butterflies flitted lazily between flowers.

A flash of red caught her eye, and she discovered a tree laden with fruit. The flesh resembled a huge, elongated peach, graduating from red, through orange and green.

Hardly daring to believe her good fortune, she picked one and sniffed it, then took a tentative bite and groaned in happiness as the sweet, familiar taste of mango filled her mouth. She'd tried this tropical fruit in Brazil, and it had quickly become one of her favorites.

Filled with excitement, she picked four of the ripest fruits and hurried back to the beach.

She didn't have enough hands to carry all the mangos, shells, and coconuts, but she was reluctant to make another trip in the smothering heat. Pushing aside her natural embarrassment, she placed everything in the bottom half of her chemise, and lifted the hem to form a rudimentary sling.

She kept the material as low as possible, praying that Hayworth would be so busy gathering wood that he wouldn't notice her arrival, but the sound of movement stopped abruptly as she neared the camp. She looked up to find his avid gaze fixed firmly on her bare thighs.

Caro knelt as quickly as she could and deposited her bounty on the sand.

The movement seemed to snap Hayworth out of his trance, and he busied himself with covering the roof of the shelter he'd constructed in her absence. Much to her disappointment, he'd put his shirt back on, hiding all those glorious muscles of his.

"What have you got there?" he asked gruffly.

She held up a blushing fruit. "I found a mango tree."

He sent her a dubious look. "You're *sure* it's edible? The last thing we want is for one of us to get sick."

She rolled her eyes at his skepticism. "Yes, I'm sure. I've already eaten some, and I'm not frothing at the mouth or rolling around on the floor in agony. We ate these all the time in Brazil."

She pushed some lumps of driftwood together to make a rudimentary table and set the mangoes and coconuts on it, then held up more of her discoveries.

"We can use these empty coconut shells as cups for water, and these big seashells as spoons, or even plates."

"Good work."

She squashed down the glow of happiness his praise produced in her chest. "That looks like a good shelter."

He grunted, as if unimpressed with his work. "It'll do for now. It's off the ground, at least. And it should keep off the worst of the rain. It's hard not having an axe or a saw to cut branches."

"It looks wonderful," Caro said, genuinely impressed at what he'd constructed.

A few years ago, she would have bet her life on Max Cavendish not being able to put his own boots on without assistance, but his time in the army had clearly given him skills the average aristocrat did not possess.

He made a theatrical sweep of his arm. "Welcome to Chateau Cavendish, mademoiselle. The finest residence this side of Madagascar."

Caro smiled at his teasing, self-deprecating humor. The 'chateau' was a basic A frame of branches and leaves supported at the far end by three huge boulders. "It's certainly the finest edifice on *this island*," she said judiciously.

"May I give you a tour?"

"Please do."

"The floor, as you see, is the very latest in split bamboo construction, with a generous covering of palm fronds."

Caro bit her lip to stop a laugh escaping. She schooled her expression into one of mock gravity, as if she were being given a tour of one of England's finest mansions. "I believe the great architect Robert Adam uses exactly the same materials."

His lips quirked.

"And the roof?" she queried.

"The finest timber-frame, secured with vines, finished with the highest quality overlapping leaves."

Caro tapped her lips with her finger, as if giving it serious consideration. "Such an innovative technique. I'll be sure to mention it to my cousin Tristan when we're back in England. He's an architect, too."

Hayworth gestured grandly at their surroundings. "The lady will note the agreeable aspect to the south, and the unparalleled sea view."

"Magnificent," Caro crooned.

"There's the very latest in alfresco dining." He waved at her impromptu table. "And let us not forget the innovative arrangement of the facilities for personal hygiene."

"The what?"

"There aren't any chamber pots," he said, straight faced. "You're going to have to go round the back of that tree."

Caro flushed but still chuckled at his bawdy humor. She appreciated the attempt to put her at ease.

He pointed at the stream. "Not to mention the hot and cold running water."

She lifted her brows. "Hot *and* cold?"

He smiled again, and her heart gave another little jolt. He was irresistible when he was teasing.

"Hot in the afternoon when the sun's been on it. Cold in the morning, for milady's ablutions."

"Ah. And how many do you think it will accommodate? I may have a guest to stay."

His eyes twinkled. "A guest, you say? Hmm. This residence is extremely compact. In fact, it might be a bit of a crush, when one's actually inside. But provided you and your guest are on friendly terms, I don't think it will pose a problem."

Caro knew her cheeks were heating at the thought of the two of them having to take shelter inside. It barely looked big enough for them to lie side by side without touching. Still, it was better than nothing.

"I'm sure we can come to an amicable arrangement," she said smoothly. "What's the asking price?"

His sparkling gaze caught hers and for a moment she was sure he was about to ask for something outrageous, like a kiss. His gaze *did* drop to her mouth for a second, before he gave a gallant shrug.

"There's been a great deal of interest, madam. Properties on this stretch of the coast are few and far between. This wonderful estate will set you back . . . two coconuts and a mango."

"Done!"

Caro brushed her hand on her shift and then stuck it out toward him to shake. He took it, and her stomach swooped as his fingers closed around hers. He gave her hand a firm squeeze to cement the 'deal', and she squashed her feeling of disappointment when he released her and let his hand drop.

She took a cooling step back.

"If you'll give me your knife, I'll cut up the mango."

CHAPTER 7

Caro sneaked furtive glances at Hayworth as he picked up one of the coconuts she'd gathered.

"So, how do we get into these then?"

"The green ones, like that one—" she pointed to one on the ground, "have a refreshing water inside them that we can drink. We should be able to open them with your knife."

He shook the one he was holding. It made a liquid, sloshing sound. "And these darker ones? Do they have the nut inside?"

"Yes. But you have to pull off the outer husk to get to it. Without a decent blade, the best way is probably to hit it with a rock until you can peel it off."

"Right."

He set off for the water's edge and she watched as he wedged the coconut between two boulders. Then he selected another large rock, lifted it to shoulder height, and dropped it onto the top of the nut with a loud crack.

He repeated the action several times, and eventually pulled the hairy covering free. He held up the resulting nut in triumph, as if he'd captured the enemy's standard during a battle.

"Success!"

Caro smiled at his enthusiasm. For all his sophistication when he was in the *Ton*, she had the feeling that she was finally getting a glimpse of the real Max Cavendish. The man who lurked beneath the civilized, cynical veneer. A man who took a simple, primitive pleasure in doing something so physical.

A man she found extraordinarily attractive, damn it.

He strode back up the beach, clutching his prize. The coconut looked surprisingly small in his big hands.

"Now what?"

Caro took it from him and balanced it carefully between her knees. "If we open it up, we can drink the milk that's inside." She located the three darker spots on the top, and used the tip of the penknife to bore a small hole. She held it up toward him. "Try it."

"Oh no, ladies first, I insist."

She gave a wry smile. "You just want to make sure it's drinkable."

He grinned. "Maybe."

Caro put the coconut to her lips and took a sip, savoring the sweet, refreshing taste. Then she held it out for Hayworth, and her stomach clenched a little as he placed his mouth directly over the same spot hers had been without even wiping the surface.

His throat bobbed as tipped his head back and swallowed, and she clenched her fingers into a fist against the desire to reach out and touch his skin.

"Ahh," he sighed. "Now. Shall I bash this open?"

She waved him back toward the rocks. "Bash away." She *almost* finished with 'Your Grace,' but stopped herself just in time.

By the time he returned, she'd sliced up two of the mangos, and they sat on opposite logs with her makeshift table between them. Caro used the knife to hack out a few chunks of the white coconut meat from the split shell.

"I've never had mango before," Hayworth said, taking a slice. "At least, I don't *think* I have. Who knows, maybe I've eaten mango every day for weeks and don't remember? I presumably ate mango in Madagascar?"

Caro rolled her eyes, still not entirely convinced he wasn't playing an elaborate hoax on her. "Indeed, you did. Perhaps the taste will remind you. It's a little like a peach, only sweeter, with more juice."

She watched in fascination as he took a tentative bite, unable to tear her eyes away from his mouth.

His lips had always drawn her. They were firm and finely molded, and she'd spent far too many nights wondering what they would feel like pressed against her own. The juice from the mango coated the lower one in a wet sheen, and she had the sudden insane urge to lean forward and lick it off, to taste the sticky sweetness on him.

The heat was clearly making her delirious.

"Delicious," he murmured, and she glanced up to find his eyes fixed on her.

For a moment she imagined he was describing *her*, and unbidden heat flooded her cheeks. Flustered, she popped a sliver of mango between her own lips and concentrated on the heady perfume and fragrant flesh.

"Don't eat too much, or you'll get stomach ache," she murmured, between chews.

He raised his brows. "That sounds like the voice of experience."

She nodded. "Lenore once bet her favorite ribbon that I couldn't eat three in one sitting. I proved her wrong—but I wish I hadn't. I spent the rest of the day in bed, feeling terrible."

He chuckled at her wry expression.

Suddenly uncomfortable with his gaze, she glanced out at the horizon. The sun, already past its zenith and on the descent, was visible, but the patchy clouds precluded any rays that could be used to start a fire.

"It's a shame the sun isn't coming out," she grumbled. "It would be nice to get a fire going."

Hayworth stood and rinsed his hands in the stream. "Well, I for one think we've had a very successful first day, all things considered. We've found water and food. And we've got somewhere to sleep. I'd say we make a good team."

Caro shrugged, even though she was secretly thrilled at his praise. She'd never thought to hear him say something so complimentary. In fact, she suddenly realized she'd become accustomed to men viewing her as some sort of overeducated freak—a woman with far too many 'unfeminine' skills and not enough 'desirable' traits like simpering ignorance and a willingness to laugh at a man's jokes, however feeble.

"We've been incredibly fortunate," she said levelly. "I don't know what we would have done if there hadn't been fresh water." She glanced back along the beach, toward the rocky headland. "I hope the others have been so lucky."

"I'd be surprised if they hadn't. That other island looks bigger than this one, and they might even be able to row back to the ship and save the supplies that are on it. We can walk back around and see, if you like."

"Very well."

They set off, with Caro clambering over the rocks this time, since she still wore her boots. She squinted over at the island on the horizon, and gave a gasp as she spied a flicker of light.

"They've made a fire! Look!"

CHAPTER 8

A plume of smoke rose against the sky, and Hayworth let out a long whistle. "So they have. Lucky devils. I wonder how they managed that."

Caro couldn't conceal her envious groan. "I wish we were on *that* island."

He bumped her shoulder with his own in a friendly nudge, exactly as she'd seen him do with her brother. "Oh, come now. It's not so bad here. We're alive, aren't we? *'Dum Spiro Spero'*, and all that."

"While I breathe, I hope?"

He looked suitably impressed by her ability to translate the Latin, and she quashed a little spark of pride. Her Latin was excellent, thanks to her father's need for help in classifying his various butterfly species.

"Exactly. One of those crusty old Romans said it. Cicero, maybe? Or Herodotus. Either way, it was something I told myself every day when I was in Portugal. Each time I lived to see another sunset—no matter how hungry, or hurting, or tired—it was a reminder that at least I wasn't dead. Dead is final. Alive, there's a chance you'll see home again, see the people you care about. The people you love."

Caro glanced at him, surprised and oddly touched that he'd shared something so personal with her. She'd always thought of him as invincible; the untouchable, unruffled Duke of Hayworth. It was rather comforting to know that he was human, and prone to the same fears and insecurities as she herself. It made her admire him even more.

Ugh. Why couldn't he have stayed all irritating and aloof, as he'd always been in the past?

She forced herself to give a light, teasing laugh. "*Love?* I didn't think gentlemen believed in love. Will always swore he'd never fall prey to such a ridiculous emotion. He says love is only for women and fools."

Hayworth slanted her an enigmatic look. "I used to think the same, but war changes a man. I hope to find a woman to love me, flawed as I am." He stopped abruptly on the sand. "Wait! I'm not *married,* am I? I haven't a wife back in England? A fiancée? A mistress?"

Caro laughed. If he was only pretending to have lost his memory, he was doing an admirable job of it. "You do not have a wife. Nor a fiancée, as far as I know. You didn't have one when I left for Brazil eight months ago, at least."

He heaved a sigh of apparent relief.

"As to a mistress," she couldn't resist teasing, even though the topic would have been distinctly off-limits under normal circumstances, "you could well have one of those. Or several. I wouldn't know."

He'd definitely had paramours in the past. The rumor mill in the *Ton* was always whispering about him. Her heart gave a jealous little squeeze in her chest.

"I don't suppose many women want to marry an ex-soldier, turned groomsman and valet," he said evenly.

She almost snorted. She knew a hundred women who'd marry him, even if he didn't have a penny to his name. The man looked like a Greek god. And he had a title. That alone made him matrimonial gold. Add an obscene amount of money to the mix, and it was a miracle he hadn't been snapped up already.

Hayworth seemed to be expecting a response, so she feigned a look of sympathy. "You'll get back on your feet. Who knows? In a year or two you might even be promoted to stablemaster."

"Assuming we ever get off this island."

They both gazed enviously over at the glowing orange flames. Hayworth waved, and received an answering signal from a figure on the shore.

He bent and started gathering an armful of driftwood. "We should prepare our own signal fire. That way, when a ship comes, we'll be ready."

Caro nodded, pleased with his confidence that she would, indeed, be able to make a spark for them soon. His belief in her abilities was heartening. So many men she knew would have tried to do the task themselves, or dismissed her idea out of hand, and insisted on trying a hundred other ways to start a fire.

They spent the next half hour stacking a pyramid of driftwood beneath the trees, then made their way back to camp.

The sun was slipping closer to the horizon, and the sky was beginning to turn a gorgeous mix of purples and pinks. It was going to be a spectacular sunset. Caro began collecting more driftwood in readiness for the morning, but Hayworth ventured to the water's edge.

"I'm going for a swim."

He tugged off his shirt and threw it up onto the dry rocks.

"You might want to look away, Miss Montgomery," he warned with a low laugh, "because I am about to remove my breeches."

Caro sucked in a breath and willed herself to turn and face the shelter, even though every fiber of her being wanted to turn around and peek. Her ears strained to hear the rasp of fabric being shed, then she heard the splash as he waded out into the shallows.

A larger splash, and she heard him call, "You can turn around now."

She did so, and pretended she was perfectly used to seeing a partially submerged, naked man swimming in the sea not fifty paces from her.

Despite the clearness of the water, the lengthening shadows and unhelpful movement of the waves prevented her from seeing more than the briefest flashes of skin. But just the knowledge that he was there, *perfectly naked*, was enough to make her feel decidedly on edge.

The rosy glow of the setting sun gilded his broad shoulders and set the droplets of water in his hair sparkling. He ducked beneath the surface and reappeared, running his hands through his wet hair like some mythical merman, or Poseidon, emerging from the deep to claim a mortal lover from the land.

Caro could quite see how a girl might be tempted. The curve of his biceps and ridged perfection of his chest made her mouth run dry. The suspicion that he might be flaunting himself deliberately, to try to attract her, formed in her brain, but she dismissed it almost immediately. A man like Hayworth would never be interested in a woman like her.

"Are you coming in?" he demanded playfully. "You must be hot."

Caro was decidedly warm – and not just from collecting the wood. She would have loved to take a refreshing dip, but there was no way she was going to take off any more clothing in Hayworth's distracting presence.

"Maybe tomorrow. May hair will take too long to dry without the sun, and I can't sleep if it's wet."

She doubted she'd be doing much sleeping at all, with that divine body right next to her in that ridiculously small shelter, but that was beside the point.

Hayworth sent her a chiding look that suggested she was a spoilsport, but she forced herself to cross to the stream instead and wash her face and hands. She kept her back turned when he finally left the water, and waited until he'd had ample time to dress before she looked at him again.

They ate the remaining mangoes as the light began to fade and the purple shadows lengthened.

"Tomorrow, we should try to walk around the island and see how big it is." Hayworth said, and Caro had a flash of what he must have been like as a Captain in the army, planning the next day's excursions into enemy territory.

"Then we can venture inland," he continued, unaware of her perusal. "We can follow this stream and see where it leads. There might be a lake or larger river further up the hill that we can wash our clothes in. Salt water leaves them all crunchy."

Caro nodded. "Yes. It would be nice to bathe in fresh water. We can look for more food, too. I remember where my mango tree is, but there will probably be others."

"You don't have to come," he offered. "It might be quite strenuous."

"Ha! I'll wager I've crossed more difficult terrain than you have, Max Cavendish. I once had to cross a river while balancing between two suspended ropes. I'm not some simpering debutante who's never been farther afield than Brighton."

His mouth quirked in appreciation. "You're an extraordinary woman, Caroline Montgomery. Which is why I can honestly say there's no one I'd rather be shipwrecked with than you."

Caro scoffed at his blatant attempt to butter her up. She didn't believe him for a minute—no doubt he would have preferred to be marooned with one of his mistresses, who would have offered him the most basic of human comforts. But her heart still glowed at his praise. It was nice to be considered competent, at least.

"So," Hayworth said. "Time for bed?"

CHAPTER 9

"Which side do you prefer?" Hayworth asked cheerfully.

Caro's heart began to pound. She had no idea *which* side she preferred, never having shared a bed with anyone—a fact Hayworth must surely know, or at least assume, since she was clearly a lady—but she refused to let him needle her.

"The right," she said.

His smile widened. "That's good. Because I prefer the left."

She glared at him and crossed her arms defensively over her chest. "You do realize that this shelter is the *only* thing we'll be sharing tonight, Maximillian Cavendish. I'm not some London trollop you can—" she paused, unsure quite where she'd been going with that sentence.

"—use for bodily warmth?" he supplied with a laugh. "Seduce into a quivering pile of limbs?"

"Something like that," she muttered.

He lifted both hands up in a gesture of innocence. "I swear, I'll be the perfect gentleman."

"Well, good."

Caro stalked to the rocks and retrieved her dress and petticoats. Both had dried, so she went behind a bush and put her dress back on, then rolled her petticoats up into a bundle to use as a pillow. Her stays were also dry, but she couldn't face the thought of putting them back on to sleep, even if they would provide an extra layer of protection. She left them hanging on the bush.

When she emerged, Hayworth was already lying in the shelter, looking out, so she removed her boots and crawled in beside him, stockinged feet first.

The two of them lay side by side on their stomachs, supported on their elbows, and looked out at the darkening sea. Their shoulders almost touched.

"It shouldn't get too cold, even without a fire," he said. "But if, at any time, you feel the need for extra body heat, you only have to ask."

Caro gave an amused little snort. "I'm sure I'll be fine."

She tucked her petticoat pillow under her head and turned her back to him, but despite her physical exhaustion, her mind refused to calm. She'd shared a tent with her sisters, on occasion, but she'd never slept this close to a man.

In the enclosed space she could smell him—a pleasant mix of salt-clean skin and some indefinable masculine scent that made her toes curl in her stockings. The even sound of his breathing and the various rustlings of the leaves as he tried to make himself comfortable filled her ears and made her very aware of the crowded space.

Some part of him brushed her bottom, and she wriggled away, glad that he wouldn't be able to see her pink cheeks.

"Sorry," he muttered.

Caro yawned. The floor of the hut was not at all comfortable; she was going to have bruises on her hip and shoulder by the morning. Willing herself to relax, she closed her eyes and had just begun to doze when a loud 'thump' nearby made her jolt back awake with a start.

"What was that?" she yelped, her heart racing.

"Falling coconut," Hayworth muttered, apparently less alarmed than herself. "Told you we shouldn't build under the palms."

It was almost fully dark now, but the moon was out, and Caro could make out a bank of clouds above them. With a sudden patter, a barrage of raindrops began to fall, slowly at first, and then in a steady rhythmic hiss all around.

"Oh, wonderful," Hayworth groaned dryly. "Just what the doctor ordered."

Caro moved deeper into the shelter, away from the drips that now fell from the open entrance. She waited for more to start falling in through the leafy 'roof', but Hayworth must have done a decent job of covering it because no water managed to seep in.

Relieved that at least they would stay relatively dry, she closed her eyes again, oddly soothed by the sound of the rain hitting the leaves and the reassuring male presence next to her. Some primal, base part of her felt infinitely safe with Hayworth at her side. That, in itself, was a troublesome thought, but she was too tired to dissect it.

"Good night, Cavendish," she murmured.

There was a smile in his voice as he answered. "Good night, Montgomery. Sweet dreams."

CHAPTER 10

When Caro awoke, she frowned at the slanted patch of leaves in front of her nose for a few moments, utterly disoriented. Her whole body ached, and she had a vague recollection of being cold in the night, but now she felt deliciously warm—at least along the back side of her body.

The rosy glow of sunrise warmed the inside of the shelter and recollection returned with a flash of alarm. The heavy weight slung over her waist was *Hayworth's arm*. The pleasantly warm feeling behind her was *his body*, pressed against hers, full length.

Caro sucked in a scandalized breath. *Was Hayworth already awake?*

She strained her ears, her heart pounding, and identified strong, even breathing that suggested he was still deeply asleep.

Thank the Lord! She had no memory of how they'd ended up in this situation, but they'd clearly become entwined at some point during the night.

Her cheeks heated in mortification, even as she tried to stay absolutely still to catalogue the extraordinary sensations.

He was hard, and warm, and all-encompassing. He was pressed against her back so closely she could feel the rise and fall of his chest as he breathed, and the tickle of his exhalations against her neck. His knee was pressed against the back of her leg, and—oh, God!—her bottom was nestled quite wonderfully in the lee of his lap.

She'd never in her life expected to wake in his arms. Hayworth undoubtedly had no idea of what he was doing; he was probably so used to sharing a bed with a woman that his body had automatically reached out to hers in the night.

Determined to extricate herself from this mortifying situation, she slid out of his embrace as quietly as possible. She paused, pulse racing, when he mumbled something incoherent and rolled over onto his back, but thankfully he did not wake.

When she was fully out of the shelter, she risked a glance back at him, giving into the urge to watch him as he slept. It was such a privilege, a secret moment she'd keep with her forever. The dawn's rays highlighted the slope of his nose and the stubble on his cheek. Caro took one last longing glance and forced herself to go for a head-clearing walk up the beach.

She felt more awake when she'd taken off her stockings and paddled in the sea. She gathered a few more coconuts, and when she returned to camp it was to find Hayworth sitting on an upturned log with his penknife in one hand and her stays in the other.

She dropped the coconuts and rushed toward him.

"Hoi! What on earth are you doing?"

He continued merrily ripping through the stitching of her stays with the blade. "I'm taking them apart so we can use the steel wires to make a fish hook."

Caro's whole body flushed at seeing her private underwear in his big hands. "What? No!"

"You're going to have to make sacrifices for survival. You can either have fish for dinner or a well-supported bosom. Which is it to be?"

His unrepentant gaze flickered to her breasts, and Caro

cursed the way her nipples seemed to tingle in response. She crossed her arms in front of her. "Fine. Fish."

"Good choice," he grinned, even though she hadn't really been given a choice at all. With a rip and a tug, he pulled one of the thin metal strips from its setting, and proceeded to bend it into a curve. With his knife he cut it down to size and sharpened the end into a point.

"What are you going to use for string?" Caro groused.

He pointed behind him, at her petticoats, and she cursed herself for leaving them behind. She should have known better than to trust him with anything.

"I've already pulled a good long piece of thread from the bottom," he said, clearly relishing her displeasure. "Don't worry, it's still perfectly wearable."

With an irritated huff, Caro sank down onto her own piece of driftwood. The sun had risen, but clouds dotted the sky. Still, there was hope that they might disperse as the day wore on. She might be able to make a fire after all.

She nibbled on a bit of coconut and watched with silent appreciation as Hayworth set about making a rudimentary fishing pole from a stick, the length of cotton thread, and his newly-made hook.

Not wanting to be accused of idleness, she wandered to the rocks and inspected the rock pools, then pried a limpet from its home. She tried to catch some crabs, but the little devils were too fast.

"Here," she held the limpet out to Hayworth. "You'll be needing something for bait."

His smile of thanks made her stomach somersault. She told herself it was hunger, not attraction.

She'd thought he'd try to catch something immediately, but instead he placed the rod inside the shelter. "No point catching a fish until we have a fire to cook it on. I don't fancy eating it raw." He glanced at the sky. "When those clouds move off, we can try your idea with the watch. Until then, how about we follow the stream inland?"

"Excellent plan."

Caro pulled on her boots, and he did the same, and together they set off into the trees, following the trickle of water.

The land started to rise almost immediately, and they were forced to scramble up muddy banks and rocky outcrops. Tangled tree roots provided countless handholds, but wet leaves and slippery slopes made progress slow.

They found the place where their trickle split off from a larger stream, and continued following that uphill.

At one particularly rocky part Hayworth reached back and offered Caro his hand. Her heart fluttered as she took it, and she marveled at his strength as he effortlessly pulled her upward. Her attention snagged on the play of sinews in his forearm—he'd rolled the sleeves of his shirt up—but just as she was wondering what they must feel like, her foot slipped and she scraped her knee on the jagged rocks.

"Owww!" Her shout was as much annoyance at her own stupidity as it was due to pain.

"Careful!" Hayworth hauled her up the last rocks and onto more even ground.

She hopped on one leg, then grabbed a nearby tree for support as he dropped to his knees in front of her and caught her ankle.

"Hush!" he commanded, anticipating her disapproval. "Let me look."

He pushed up the bottom of her dress without waiting for permission, and she bent to inspect the damage. Her stockings had protected her knee a little, but a fair-sized scrape oozed blood, staining the ripped white cotton a deep red.

Hayworth made a clucking sound with his tongue. She wasn't sure if it was meant to be chiding or sympathetic. She winced as he scooped a handful of cold water from the stream and washed the wound, but pushed him away as soon as he'd finished his ministrations. He took his time releasing her ankle.

"Sure you don't want me to kiss it better?" he teased.

"I'm fine. It's just a scratch."

He stood and peered down at her with a frown. "I know. But you still need to tend to it. Wash it in salt water when we get back to the beach. The last thing we need is for you to get an infection out here with no access to any medicine."

Caro blushed, embarrassed by her own carelessness, and relished the sting in her knee. She deserved it for being an ogling idiot. She, more than anyone, knew that the jungle, while beautiful, could be deadly.

Hayworth, however, seemed to have forgotten his irritation. He turned his head and held his hand up as if for quiet. "Do you hear that?"

Caro frowned. She *could* hear a faint rushing sound, but she'd assumed it was the frantic beating of her heart. Now she concentrated, it was plainly audible above the general noise of the forest.

"It sounds like a waterfall," she said, excitement lifting her tone.

Hayworth caught her hand. "It does indeed. Come on!"

CHAPTER 11

With Caro in tow, Hayworth pushed through the jungle, staying close to the banks of the stream. The sound of rushing water grew ever louder until they burst out of the undergrowth and into a clearing bathed in sunlight.

"Oh, goodness!" Caro's mouth opened on a gasp of delight.

A torrent of water rushed from the top of a rocky cliff and tumbled at least thirty feet into the pool before them. A fine mist spray clouded the base of the falls, creating a permanent rainbow where the sun caught it.

"Do you think it's safe to swim?" She had to raise her voice to be heard over the sound of the water.

"I don't see why not, as long as we mind the slippery rocks." Hayworth sent her one of his irresistible grins. Before she could blink, he'd tugged off his boots and stockings, stripped off his shirt, and began making his way carefully into the pool.

Caro bit back a smile. She'd never met anyone who could undress so quickly.

He set off swimming with long strokes toward the base of the falls, his strong arms pushing against the current, then turned to face her, treading water.

"What are you waiting for?" he shouted. "I promise I won't look at your unmentionables."

To emphasize his point, he turned so his glistening shoulders faced her.

After a brief moment of indecision, Caro threw propriety to the wind. She was desperate for a swim, and the water looked incredibly inviting. She stepped behind a tree, removed everything except for her shift, and peered out at the pool. Hayworth's back was still turned, so she made her way gingerly over the rocks and into the water.

Compared to the sea, it was bracingly cold, and she shrieked as she made the final plunge. She came up for air, then ducked below the surface again, fanning her hair to rinse out every last grain of sand and salt.

"Oh, that feels so good!"

Hayworth, swimming in lazy circles across the pool, grinned at her enthusiasm. She tried to swim close to the base of the falls, as he had, but the push of the water was so strong she gave up after only a few strokes, arms aching with the effort.

She turned to find him right in front of her. Sunlight glinted off his slicked-back hair and glimmered like diamonds on his muscled shoulders. Water droplets trickled down his nose and gathered at the corners of his mouth.

Caro couldn't look away. She had the most insane urge to lick those drops from his lips, to taste the cool water on his warm skin.

He drifted closer. "Caro." His voice was a deep growl, almost a warning.

Her gaze flicked up to his. "Yes?"

"When you look at me like that—"

"Yes?" she prompted, half teasing, half terrified of what he was going to say. Her heart was pounding against her ribs, and not just because of the unaccustomed exercise.

He took a deep breath. "Never mind." A rueful smile curved

his lips as he reached out and smoothed a strand of wet hair from her cheek. "Is 'disheveled castaway' a fashion style back in London? Because if it's not, it should be. It suits you."

She let out a snort and tried to stay afloat. He was tall enough to stand, but her toes barely touched the bottom of the pool.

"Pfft. You're only saying that because there's no other woman on this whole island for you to flirt with. You, Max Cavendish, are a scoundrel."

"That may be true, but that doesn't alter the facts. You're beautiful. I've always thought so."

Caro's pulse skipped a beat, but she feigned airy amusement. "And *you've* clearly had a blow to the head that's affecting your judgment."

A wave buffeted them, and she grabbed his arm to steady herself—then immediately regretted it as the muscle flexed beneath her fingers, slick and impressively solid. Her stomach flipped, but before she could push herself away from temptation, he caught both her shoulders in his hands.

The upper part of his chest rose above the lapping water, mere inches from her own. Caro glanced down and realized she might as well have removed her chemise, for all the coverage it was providing. The cold had peaked her nipples into tight buds and their dark tips were clearly visible through the near-transparent fabric.

Heat scalded her cheeks as she realized Hayworth had noticed, as well. His sea-blue gaze roamed over her and his fingers tightened on her upper arms. For a blissful moment she thought he was going to drag her against his chest and kiss her, but he pushed himself away with an almighty splash.

She quashed a groan of disappointment.

"You should get dressed." His voice was deeper than she'd ever heard it. "I'll wait until you're done before I get out."

Thoroughly flustered, Caro nodded. She swam to the shallows and made her way out, but when she glanced back to see if

Hayworth was watching her, he was swimming with purposeful strokes to the far side of the pool.

* * *

Bloody hell.

Max ducked under that water and blew out a stream of frustrated bubbles, willing the chill of the pool to cool his ardor.

Had he really thought this place was heaven? It was hell. Pure hell. And he'd been sentenced to a never-ending state of aching, yearning lust.

He was deliberately *not* looking at Caro, but the image of her was seared into his brain. Her shift had been rendered completely sheer by the water. It looked like a sheen of icing. Her perfect breasts had reminded him of glazed buns; each with a gorgeous cherry nipple on the top begging for his mouth.

God, he wanted to taste them. To taste *her.*

He'd been a split second away from doing it, too. The interest, the invitation, in her eyes had been unmistakable, and it had sent a punch of primal satisfaction to his gut. But she was an innocent, and he would *not* seduce her until he was absolutely sure she wanted him as much as he wanted her.

His cock, however, needed no further convincing. He was as hard as an iron bar in his breeches and he couldn't leave the water until the damn thing had subsided—which was unlikely with Caro half-naked just a few paces away on the bank.

Max ducked beneath the water again and scrubbed his hair vigorously. By the time he resurfaced, slightly more in control of himself, Caro was dressed and loitering in the shade of the trees with her back turned to give him privacy.

With a resigned sigh, he waded from the water, dried himself as best he could with his shirt, and pulled it on, along with his boots and stockings. If he'd been alone, he would have swum naked—and wouldn't now be saddled with wet breeches trickling water into his boots. He sent a silent apology to his bootmaker, Hoby, back in London, who would have an apoplexy to see his finest—and most expensive—creations in such a pitiful state.

Giving Caro a wide berth, he started down the trail. "Let's get back to the beach."

They walked in silence, with Max acutely aware of her behind him, when he suddenly heard her stop.

"Max."

He turned. It was the first time she'd ever used his given name. "What's the matter?"

"Stay still and do not be alarmed."

He frowned. "What do you mean 'don't be alarmed.' That's precisely the kind of thing someone says when the other person should be *very alarmed indeed*."

Her lips curved up in an easy smile. "There's a spider on your back, that's all."

He froze, suppressing the urge to look over his shoulder or to start brushing his hands all over himself to get rid of the thing. "What kind of a spider? A big one? Get it off!"

She caught his forearm and turned him slowly back around. "It's only a little one. Here, let me."

He quelled an instinctive shudder as he felt movement on his back. He hoped to God it was her hands.

"There!"

Her confident tone lowered his pulse rate a little, but it ratcheted back up when he discovered her cupping the biggest spider he'd ever seen in his life in her hands.

He took an involuntary step back. "Bloody hell, woman! Kill it!"

She sent him a laughing glance and bent her head to address the spider.

"Oh, don't you listen to him," she crooned, as one might to a lap dog or small child. "He's just grouchy. You are *such* a *handsome* fellow, aren't you?"

Max broke out into a cold sweat. "Put it down! Are you mad?"

Caro laughed—actually laughed. The girl was out of her mind.

She raised the monstrosity up to eye level. "This is a tarantula. Rather sweet, if a little hairy. I had one as a pet in Brazil. His name was Timothy. I was very sad to leave him behind."

Max fought the need to slap it out of her hand and run screaming into the forest. "You are *not* keeping that thing as a pet. I forbid it."

With a grin, she extended her hand close to a branch and the nightmare creature slowly ambled off her skin and onto the twig.

He let out a relieved huff. "You shouldn't take such chances. What if it had bitten you?"

"Tarantulas aren't usually aggressive and rarely bite. But even if he had bitten me, I would have been fine. Have you ever been stung by a bee? It feels like that."

Max felt his jaw drop open. "You've been bitten by one *before?*"

"Just once. Timmy didn't want to share his mouse." She watched in obvious fascination as the newly-released specimen clambered up the tree. "Timmy was a lovely blue color, but this one, you see, is black and brown."

"I thought your family studied butterflies," he said hoarsely. "Pretty, harmless butterflies."

"We do. At least, father does, and we all help him. But one can't walk ten feet in a jungle without encountering things that are *not* butterflies."

Max shook his head, stoutly refusing to think about all the other *not butterflies* that might be close to him at that very moment. *Dear God.*

"Thank you for removing it," he said stiffly.

Caro sent him a beatific smile. "You're very welcome."

CHAPTER 12

Caro bit back her laugh at Max's reaction to the spider as they made their way back to the beach. For some reason the knowledge that the man who had led his troops into battle, who'd faced the horror of Napoleon's army without flinching, was afraid of spiders, was incredibly endearing.

Perhaps feeling that his masculine aura of invincibility had been tarnished, he stomped to the shelter when they reached the beach, collected his fishing pole and knife, and set off toward the promontory with a grunt about "catching us some dinner."

Caro let out a little chuckle. If anything, her admiration for him had only increased. The tarantula had been far larger than anything he would have previously encountered in England, and she'd been pleased that he'd obeyed her command to stay still, rather than flailing around and trying to dislodge it himself.

She only hoped that her unladylike display of affection for the eight-legged creature hadn't lowered her in *his* estimation. It was perfectly acceptable for a lady to like kittens or puppies, but an interest in arachnids was rather less common.

She finger-combed her damp hair in an attempt to remove some of the tangles, and when the sun broke through the clouds, her spirits lifted. She hastened to Max's jacket and pulled the watch from his pocket, then gathered the tinder necessary to start a fire.

Cross-legged, she directed the bright circle of reflected light onto a pile of shredded coconut bark, and watched in excitement as a dark spot appeared. The singed area began to smolder, and she heaped more dried grass on top of it, blowing carefully. The sudden bright flare of a flame was like a tiny miracle.

"Yes!"

Careful not to swamp the flame, she added larger twigs, and when she was sure it was past the danger point, she sat back on her bottom with a sigh of satisfaction.

A glance up the beach showed Max had his back to her; he was casting his makeshift fishing hook into the shallows. With a sudden jerk he pulled back his arm and tugged a silvery, glittering fish from the waves. He almost lost his balance trying to land the thing on the rocks, but managed it at last, and his whoop of triumph echoed across the bay.

He straightened, fish in hand, and held it up to show her—and it was then that he noticed the smoke and her fire.

Caro grinned and waved, and he waved back, leaping athletically down from the rocks and jogging back along the sand.

"You made a fire!" His sun-flushed face was wreathed in a smile. "You marvelous thing!"

"And you caught us some dinner," she countered, nodding at the fish in his hand.

"I did. I've no idea what it is, but it saves us from eating nothing but mango."

He headed back the water and made quick work of cleaning the fish, while Caro piled more wood on the fire until it was a steady blaze. When he returned, he sank to the sand next to her and held his hands out toward the flames with a sigh of satisfaction.

"Now this is excellent. We'll dine like kings tonight."

Caro stilled as a sudden thought occurred to her. "Wait, what day is it?"

He shrugged. "Don't ask me."

"We left Madagascar on December the twenty first, and the storm was the night of the twenty second. Which means we woke up on the beach here yesterday, the twenty third—"

"—which makes *today* Christmas Eve!" he finished. "Tomorrow's Christmas day."

"We're missing Christmas!"

"We're not *missing* it," he smiled. "We're just having it somewhere else, that's all. Somewhere interesting. What would you usually do? If you were in England, that is. Sing carols? Decorate the house?" His eyes twinkled. "Hang a branch of mistletoe over the doorframe, hoping for a kiss?"

He glanced up, as if expecting a similar branch to be suspended above their heads, but there was only the swaying green lattice of palm fronds. He puffed his lower lip in a disappointed pout.

"We usually spend Christmas with the family, if we're in England." Caro said. "Especially the cousins. We've been absent so often that it's lovely when we all manage to get together."

"I know your cousins. Tristan and I were at university together."

"I was sorry to miss his wedding. But father *insisted* on going to Brazil. Whoever imagined a Montgomery would fall in love with a *Davies*? First Maddie married Gryff, and then Tristan married Carys." She frowned. "Wait, you were invited to their wedding, I'm sure of it. Don't you remember?"

If he could remember Tristan's wedding, a few months ago, then surely he'd remember attending as a duke, and not as a stable hand?

"I'm still a bit hazy about England."

"I can't believe you don't remember my great aunts," she prodded. "Constance and Prudence? They're infamous in the *Ton* for their indiscretion."

He shook his head. "Sorry."

Caro breathed a silent sigh of relief. Her deception was safe—for now.

The fish, whatever it was, turned out to be delicious, and they washed it down with fresh water and mango.

By unspoken agreement they built the fire into a roaring blaze. Max withdrew a long stick from the embers, and together they carried it over the rocks, and onto the adjacent beach. Several of the *Artemis's* passengers could be seen across the strait, and Max waved the smoking torch in their general direction.

Two of them waved back, and Caro liked to think it was her father, or perhaps her mother. At least they'd know that she and Hayworth hadn't murdered each other. Yet.

The sun set as they walked back to camp, and Caro let out a jaw-cracking yawn. Max bumped his shoulder against hers.

"Early night for you, sleepyhead." He motioned to the shelter. "In you go. I'm going to stay up for a while and make sure the fire doesn't go out."

Caro didn't bother to argue. As the sun dipped beyond the horizon in an extravagant display of salmon pink and lavender, she shuffled beneath the leaves. The light from the fire was extraordinarily comforting. It flickered shadows on the sand, and she dozed, half-listening to Max moving around the clearing, and adding fuel to the fire.

"'Night Caro."

His low tones drifted through her fuzzy brain, and she managed to mumble, "'Night, Max."

Her last thought, as she drifted off to sleep, was; *When had she started thinking of him as Max, and not Hayworth?*

CHAPTER 13

Max was already up and fishing when Caro awoke. She had no recollection of him sleeping next to her at all. Had he stayed up all night with the fire? Had he decided to forgo the shelter entirely and sleep elsewhere? Was the idea of sleeping next to her so unpalatable? *She didn't snore, did she? Or smell?*

Surreptitiously, she lifted the collar of her shift and took a sniff.

She pushed away such depressing thoughts as she splashed her face and plaited her hair. This might be the most unexpected Christmas day she'd ever spent, but she would contribute her share to the day's bounty.

She gathered some mangos, then returned to the beach. Wading into the turquoise shallows, she rearranged several small rocks into a V shape that funneled into a shallow rock pool. Then she splashed about, trying to herd shoals of fish into her trap, as a farmer's dog might drive a flock of sheep.

It took numerous attempts—the fish presumably being more intelligent than sheep—but eventually six small silver-blue fish raced into the pool. She quickly closed the exit with a rock, then used her petticoats as a rudimentary net to catch them.

By the time she returned, panting, wet, but victorious, Max was cooking something over the fire. He squinted at her against the sun, and her heart gave a little thump at his rumpled, piratical appearance. Even without decent sleep and a daily shave the man was obnoxiously attractive.

"What have you there?"

"More fish. And mangos."

"I caught a lobster between the rocks." He gestured at the crustacean suspended on a stick over the fire. "Not exactly what I imagined we'd be eating for Christmas dinner, but never mind. Let's pretend we're in England, at your house, with no expense spared. What are we eating?"

Caro smiled at his attempt to stay positive. "Well, I suppose we would have roast beef, or roast duck. Roast potatoes, carrots, peas, and parsnips. And gravy, of course."

"Mmm." Max smacked his lips in appreciation and held up a coconut shell full of water. "And presumably some wine from the cellar." He took a sip, then passed it to her. "An excellent vintage."

Caro took a seat next to him by the fire and sampled the 'wine'.

"What would be for dessert?" he urged.

"Ah, well, that would be Christmas pudding."

"Set alight with brandy?"

"Of course. And topped with cream, or brandy butter, or custard."

"I'd have all three," he said solemnly.

"And if you still had room after that, then I suppose we'd have a few mince pies and a sherry."

"I feel full just thinking about it." He glanced sideways at her, and the laughter lingered in his eyes as he lifted his hand and trailed his finger down the bridge of her nose and across her cheek.

"You've caught the sun," he murmured. "You're all pink."

She flushed even more at his unexpected touch, certain she must be the same color as the lobster. Her stomach somersaulted, but she tried to brush off her nervousness with a joke.

"Oh, the shame! My vouchers to Almacks will be withdrawn."

He leaned in conspiratorially. "I'll make sure you get in."

Caro stilled. Did he realize what he'd just said? A mere stable-master wouldn't have any sway with patronesses like Lady Jersey. Such confidence could only come from the Duke of Hayworth.

Did he remember who he was?

She gazed at him suspiciously, but the intent look on his face distracted her. He hadn't lowered his hand. Instead, he slipped it around her head to cradle the back of her skull.

Caro sucked in a breath. His eyes flicked to her lips, and everything inside her tensed in wicked anticipation.

"All this talk of pudding has me craving something sweet," he murmured. "Do you know what would be sweet?"

She managed a slight shake of her head.

"Kissing you."

She couldn't frame a response. Her wits had gone begging.

"Let's just pretend there's mistletoe," he said huskily.

And then he kissed her.

For a full second Caro was so surprised that she didn't move. And then she melted against him like a candle held too close to the fire. She'd dreamed of kissing him for years, but the reality was better than she'd ever imagined.

His lips were firm, and a little rough. Caro kissed him back, inexpertly, and when his tongue slipped between her lips to tangle with her own, she gave a gasp of delight. She closed her eyes, drowning in the taste, the feel of him. Experimentally, she swirled her own tongue against his, and he groaned deep in his chest. His fingers tightened for a moment against her nape, and then he drew back.

She stared at him, panting and breathless.

"Merry Christmas," he rasped.

"Merry Christmas."

He released her head and returned his attention to the fire, as if the earth hadn't just shifted on its axis.

Caro drew her knees up to her chest and stared blindly into the flames. Her whole body was tingling and she pressed her lips together to stop herself from begging him to do it again. And again. And again.

"Oh, I almost forgot." Max reached behind him into the shelter. "I got you a present."

Caro lifted her brows. He caught her wrist and pressed something into her palm. "It's only a stone with a hole in it. I thought you could put it on a necklace or something."

A pink flush rose on his cheekbones and Caro came to the delightful realization that he was blushing.

"Thank you," she said solemnly. She closed her fingers around it, as pleased as if he'd presented her with a diamond the size of a robin's egg. "I'm sorry, I haven't got anything for you."

"That's all right."

Silence reigned as they shared the lobster, but Caro's thoughts kept returning to the kiss.

"A penny for your thoughts."

She jumped at his question and cast around for an entirely different subject. "Do you know, I promised my parents that when we got back to England, I'd start seriously considering my suitors."

His brows rose.

"But now," she continued, "even if by some miracle we *do* get rescued, I doubt I'll have any suitors to consider. Who's going to believe I'm still an innocent when I've been alone with you for so long? I'll be completely unmarriageable."

"You don't sound particularly distressed by the prospect," he observed carefully.

"Well, in all honesty, I'm not. It's not as if I've ever met a man I wanted to marry."

Caro avoided his eyes as she spouted that disgraceful lie. The one man she'd secretly dreamed of marrying was sitting right beside her on the sand.

Not that he needed to know that mortifying piece of information.

Max rubbed the stubble on his chin and looked thoughtful. "Hmm. It's true, I'm afraid. Your reputation might already be beyond repair. People love to gossip, and they'll always think the worst. Whether you're innocent or not is largely irrelevant. They'll never believe a man and a woman could spend as long as we have together in such circumstances and not be . . . intimate."

His blue eyes caught hers and held. "There's really only one thing you can do." His expression was perfectly serious.

"What's that?"

"Seduce me and make the best of it." The laughter spilled back into his eyes. "You might as well be hanged for a sheep as for a lamb."

Caro gave a choked gasp. "Are you propositioning me?"

"Of course not. That would be highly inappropriate. I'm a lowly stable hand and you're a lady. I'm suggesting *you* proposition *me*."

He sent her an amused look that also managed to make her heart beat faster in her chest, even though she knew he wasn't being serious. "I promise to be an easy conquest. You can have your wicked way with me and I won't put up any resistance at all."

Caro whacked him on the arm for his teasing and decided it was time to come clean about his true station in life.

"You're not actually a—"

"—scoundrel?" he interrupted, before she could finish. "I beg to differ. I'm having the most ungentlemanly thoughts about all the ways you can besmirch my reputation."

She shook her head, both flattered and a little scandalized.

"You're ridiculous. You'd be saying the same thing to *any* woman you were stuck here with, whether duchess or dairymaid."

He clapped his hand over his heart in a mock show of hurt. "You wound me, milady."

With a laugh to cover her fluttering pulse, she got to her feet and brushed the sand from her skirts. "I'm going to the waterfall for a swim."

Max accepted her retreat with a knowing look that suggested he knew she was running away. He picked up his pocket watch from where it rested on a piece of driftwood, flicked open the lid, and glanced at the dial.

"If you're not back in an hour I'll assume you've been eaten by tarantulas and send out a search party."

"You'd brave such monsters to come looking for me?"

His lips quirked, but his expression was somehow earnest. "If I thought you'd show your appreciation in a suitably enthusiastic manner—" His gaze on her lips left no doubt that he was talking about kissing, "Then yes. I think I'd brave anything at all."

Flustered yet again, Caro took her leave.

As she stomped through the forest toward the waterfall, she tried to remember all the reasons she shouldn't be flirting with Maximillian Cavendish, but his teasing words kept swirling around her brain.

He was right. She *would* be judged when she got back to England. Rumors would fly, and the more she and her family tried to protest her innocence, the more people would suspect the worst.

If this escapade had really rendered her unmarriageable, then why *shouldn't* she satisfy her curiosity about lovemaking? Fate had stranded her with the only man she'd ever desired, and he seemed perfectly willing to seduce her, or to allow himself to be seduced.

If she was doomed to a life of spinsterhood for the rest of her days, why shouldn't she seize this chance to experience real passion, just once?

CHAPTER 14

"Bloody woman."

Max strode up the hill toward the waterfall, muttering under his breath. She'd been away for far longer than her allotted hour, and his heart pounded as he alternated between frustration and worry.

What if she'd had an accident? What if she'd slipped on the rocks and broken her ankle, or cracked her head?

He increased his pace, his thighs burning as he pushed through the trees and burst into the clearing, braced to either rescue her, or to scold her for needlessly worrying him.

His words died on his lips.

Caro was still in the pool.

Naked.

Max was quite sure his heart stopped beating before roaring back to life.

He checked the pile of white cotton at his feet—yes, her shift was definitely there, along with her petticoats and dress—then he glanced back up at the undeniable flash of pale skin beneath the rippling water.

His brain went a little fuzzy.

Years of ingrained gentlemanly conduct urged him to turn around, immediately, and give her some privacy.

Years of desiring the bloody woman had him staying precisely where he was.

Cara turned in the water and saw him, and he braced himself for shrieks of maidenly outrage, but instead she started toward him with slow, deliberate strokes.

He was utterly incapable of looking away. He'd seen countless naked women, but never *her,* and his gaze flickered over her pale limbs, so teasingly suggested by the moving water that alternately cloaked and revealed.

She met his eyes as she reached the shallows, and he experienced the stab in the gut her direct look always gave him. He opened his mouth to apologize, but before he could say a word her lips quirked up in a devilish smile.

"You should come in," she said softly.

He coughed to clear his throat. "That's . . . probably not a good idea."

She tilted her head, as if considering. "I won't tell anyone if you don't."

The naughty, teasing note in her voice had him panting in disbelief. His blood was a dull roar in his ears, his cock already hard in his breeches.

"You've been longer than an hour," he growled, trying to look stern.

"I know."

Not even an apology, damn her, for worrying him.

She lifted her hand, beckoning him like a siren, and like the poor sailors of the Odyssey, he couldn't resist. Almost in a trance, he stripped off his boots and his shirt and started forward in his breeches, then stopped when she shook her head and tilted her chin at his lower half.

"Off with them, Cavendish. This is no time to be missish. Can't have you catching a fever gadding about in wet clothes, can we?"

His blood rose at her mocking repetition of his own words.

Little minx. What game was she playing? Did she think he'd be immune to her nakedness? Was this some ridiculous, misguided way of proving to herself that he didn't truly desire her? If so, she was in for a rude awakening. He'd never wanted anyone more in his life.

He sent her a dark look, a warning not to play with fire, and rested one hand casually at the top button of his falls.

"You want me to remove these?"

"I do."

He made one last, desperate attempt to make her see reason. She wasn't a complete innocent. She had to know what she was inviting. What she was risking.

"Have you ever seen a naked man, Caro?"

A delicate flush mottled her cheeks, but she held his gaze.

"An *aroused* naked man?" he pushed.

Her eyes widened, but she didn't back down. "No. But I want to."

His heart skipped another beat.

He shouldn't. He absolutely—

She stood up.

The water was only waist deep. She emerged, wet and glistening; shoulders, breasts, the sinful curve of her waist.

Oh, God. She was perfection. Pale, creamy skin, pink-tipped breasts, water droplets sliding over her like little pearls.

Maybe he'd truly died and gone to heaven. Maybe he'd been bitten by some hideous snake or terrible spider and was even now hallucinating this exquisite, deliberate provocation.

She didn't lift her hands to cover her breasts. Instead, she stood there, letting him look his fill.

"Caro," he croaked, desperate.

Her mouth curved. "I'm seducing you, Cavendish. In case you haven't noticed."

"Oh, believe me, I've noticed. What I'm wondering is why?"

"Why not?" she countered. "It was your idea. And besides, nobody has to know."

There was challenge in her tone, daring him to disagree, and a flash of annoyance warmed him. He didn't want to be her secret experiment, some nameless fling she could forget as soon as they were rescued.

He wanted forever.

But his thoughts scattered as she leaned back in the water and pushed off, and his fingers unbuttoned his breeches without consulting his brain. He shucked the fabric down his thighs, kicked them off, and dove into the water.

The invigorating chill did nothing to cool his ardor. The moment he resurfaced Caro threw herself at him and he almost went under again at the feel of her naked body pressed against his.

Her arms slid around his neck, the hard tips of her breasts squashed against his chest, and he groaned aloud in pleasure.

He was lost.

It was the most natural thing in the world to wrap his own arms around her, to urge her legs around his waist, using the buoyancy of the water to maximum effect.

God, the slip-slide feel of skin on skin was almost his undoing.

His erection was trapped between them, pressed against his stomach, and, impassioned, he caught the back of her head and pulled her in for a soul-stealing kiss.

This was nothing like the slow, leisurely exploration of before. This was openmouthed and hungry, hot and wet. She moaned into his mouth as he devoured her, holding nothing back, showing her the full force of his need.

It should have scared her. Should have had her pulling back in alarm. But Caroline Montgomery had never done the expected. She fisted the wet hair at the back of his head and tugged him closer, kissing him back as if her life depended on it.

God, she was a fast learner. Each time he angled his head to get a better taste, she angled hers the opposite way, fusing them together, giving more. Taking it all.

Unable to help himself, he traced his hand down the curve of her back and cupped her backside, squeezing the rounded flesh until she was squirming against him.

"God, Caro. Let me pleasure you. Please." He panted it against her neck.

She pressed frantic kisses along his jawline, then leaned back in his arms. "Yes."

His heart thundered in relief.

"Not here," he managed. He surged for the shallows, and she clung to him like a starfish. He carried her from the pool, barely making it to their discarded pile of clothes before he lowered her to the ground and pressed her beneath him for another mind-numbing kiss.

Scarcely able to believe it was happening, he kissed his way down her throat, then licked the water droplets from her skin as he moved lower. His hand cupped her left breast while his mouth found the right, and he relished the choked little gasp that escaped her as he swirled his tongue around her peaked nipple.

"Max!"

He opened his mouth and took more of her, his senses reeling at the taste. Sweet and clean, like the water. Bright, like sunlight.

She caught the back of his head, tugging him closer with a wordless plea. He chuckled. "You like that, Caro?"

"Oh, yes!"

His entire body was on fire, desperate for her, but he couldn't forget that she was a virgin. He had to slow down, to make it good for her. He stroked her sleek curves, shaping her ribs, her waist, her thighs. Breathing pleas and praises against her skin.

"You're beautiful, Caro."

He slid his hand over her stomach then down, into the springy triangle of hair. She tensed for a moment, and he waited for her to push him away, but instead she arched her back and tugged him closer still. He kissed her, long drugging kisses, as his fingers slid between her legs to toy with her folds. She was wet, both from the water and her own excitement, and his heart hammered in his chest at the proof of her desire.

She wanted him. *Finally.*

He slipped his finger into her, just a little, and she gasped, then writhed against him. In and out, slowly, showing her the way. He swirled his thumb over the hard little bead at the top of her sex, teasing her mercilessly, and she cried out against his throat, arching into him. Her hands roamed his skin, clutching at his shoulders, his back, his arms, but he was too intent on bringing her to her first crisis to fully savor her touch.

Her breathing hitched and he quickened the pace, pushing deeper, loving the little sounds of pleasure that escaped her. Was she pretending he was a stable hand? Or the Duke of Hayworth, having his wicked way with her? It didn't matter. He was Max, and she was Caro, and he'd wanted to do this to her for a thousand years.

She was hot, and slick, her inner muscles clutching at him, and for a split second he considered withdrawing his hand and sliding his cock inside her instead.

No. This time wasn't for him. And he couldn't risk her getting pregnant, either.

He claimed her mouth, thrusting his tongue in a wicked counterpoint to the movement of his hand, and she surged against him.

"Let it happen, sweeting," he whispered against her lips. "Chase it."

"Oh!"

He felt her climax with a rush of primal satisfaction. Her body squeezed his fingers as she arched up, riding the waves of pleasure with a cry that echoed around the clearing and sent birds flapping from the trees.

When it was over, she simply collapsed. Her arms flopped to the ground and her limbs went lax, and for a moment he feared she'd passed out. And then she let out a sigh of pure happiness and nestled her head beneath his chin.

"My God, no wonder nobody tells young ladies about this," she breathed in awed tones. "There wouldn't be a virgin left in England if they knew how lovely ruination feels."

Max propped himself on his elbows and smiled down at her. Her face was flushed, her skin dewy, and his heart gave a funny little flip inside his chest.

His cock still throbbed in painful urgency, but he smoothed her hair away from her face with a gentle hand. "Nice?"

She sent him an incredulous, laughing look. "More than nice. Astonishing. Thank you."

He bit back a smile at her earnestness. "Thank *you*," he echoed solemnly. "One does one's best to help a damsel in distress. You were clearly drowning and in need of rescue."

Her clear gaze met his as she turned on her side to face him. "But what about you?" Her hand stroked his shoulder, then trailed with casual devastation down over his chest. She flattened her palm directly over his pounding heart. There was no chance that she wouldn't be able to feel it.

"What about me?" he drawled.

She bit her lip and took a deep breath as if steeling herself, then slid her hand down over the muscled ridges of his abdomen and into the line of hair that arrowed from his navel to his groin.

"I think *you* need rescuing, too. Show me what to do."

CHAPTER 15

Max caught Caro's wrist to slow her southward exploration.

"You don't need to do that. I'm fine."

Her eyes twinkled as she slid a sly, frankly curious look down between their bodies. "You don't look fine," she said with a laugh that made his toes curl. "You look . . . uncomfortable. *Swollen*, even."

"It'll go down," he growled. "Just—"

He hissed to a stop, his mind suddenly blank as she slid her fingers around his cock and squeezed gently.

"Oh, my," she breathed in wonder. "Does that hurt?"

Max ground his teeth against the blinding urge to thrust into her hand. "No, but—"

She opened her fingers and stroked him, and her touch sent bolts of lightning shooting up his spine.

"Show me how to please you. It's only fair."

With a groan, Max gave in. Gazing deep into her eyes, he reached down, caught her hand, and showed her how to hold him. He wrapped his own fingers around hers and watched her eyes widen as she caught the rhythm.

It didn't take long. The feel of her, the scent of her filling his nose, the soft touch of her hand—the combination undid him. After only a few strokes his stomach muscles tensed, and with a smothered cry he pulsed in her hand, spending himself against his stomach.

She didn't seem to be disgusted. She watched him with a kind of fascinated interest, and he realized with a flash of humor that it was the same look she'd given that damned tarantula; awe mingled with respect.

With a chuckle he rolled over and sat up, then went to wash himself in the pool. When he returned, she'd pulled her dress over her nakedness and he bit back a disappointed huff.

"You could have stayed naked. There's no-one else to see."

Her cheeks were a becoming pink, and he wondered if she was embarrassed or, worse, regretting what they'd just done, but then she sent him a cheeky smile of her own.

"True, but it's not very practical if we encounter a *real* serpent." She sent a meaningful glance at his crotch. "Or another spider."

Max pulled his breeches on with a grin. "You're right. Sunburn might be a problem too. Clothes it is."

* * *

CARO HAD to force herself to look away from the golden, muscled perfection of Max's body. A body that had just introduced her an incredible new world of pleasure.

Even though she was dressed again, she felt naked, stripped bare by the astonishingly intimate things they'd just done.

She told herself there was no need to be embarrassed. She was a scientist, after all. She would treat the past half hour as an interesting physical experiment. She could be cool, mature, sophisticated. Like his previous lovers.

As Max donned his shirt and boots, Caro tugged on the rest

of her clothes and followed him down the hill, silently drinking in the breadth of his shoulders and the beautiful curves of his backside.

She'd been touching him mere moments ago. Already it seemed unreal, like a fever-dream, and yet her every step made her aware of the new sensitivity of her skin; the cotton shift brushing her breasts, the unexpected ache between her thighs.

She'd made a mistake in allowing Max to touch her. Instead of satisfying her curiosity about lovemaking, as she'd hoped, it had done the exact opposite.

She wanted more.

There *was* more, too. She'd been around farm animals long enough to know that the male put his member *inside* the female. She pressed her fist to the center of her chest and tried to ignore the ache that throbbed beneath her skin. What would *that* feel like?

She tore her eyes from the tempting curls at the back of Max's head, and turned her attention to the lush green forest instead.

"Max, wait."

He stilled immediately. "Oh, God, no. Don't tell me it's another spider. Because if it is, I—"

"No, it's a nice surprise. Look." She pointed upward. "Bananas."

A relieved smile broke out on his face. "That is *much* better than a spider."

With the help of a fallen tree, he detached a bunch of the yellow-green fruit and as he jumped down Caro realized she was grinning at him like a simpleton. A shocking possibility dawned on her.

Dear God, was she *in love with him*?

She'd always found him attractive, always enjoyed their sparring and craved their interactions, but this warm, glowing satisfaction whenever she was in his presence was new.

He was so much more than just his title. He was an aristocrat who wasn't afraid to get his hands dirty, a gorgeous, physical specimen who, astonishingly, appreciated her and her myriad eccentricities.

He was, in fact, everything she wanted in a man; strong, amusing, protective, resourceful, intelligent.

Oh, she was in so much trouble.

"We should take some of the leaves, too," she said, mainly to distract herself. "We can use them on the roof of the shelter. They'll be much better than the palm fronds."

Max dutifully collected an armful of the large, flat leaves, and they set off.

Caro was silent as they walked back down the beach, and it was only Max's shout that finally snapped her out of her brooding.

"Hoi, come look at this!"

He was at the high tide mark, standing over a large brown spherical object. It was quite a bit larger than a coconut, and Caro smiled at his bemused expression.

"It's a coco de mer nut," she said. "I saw one in Madagascar, at the King's palace. They're extremely rare."

Max tilted his head. "It looks just like—"

"—a woman's bare bottom?" she finished with a smile. "Yes, it does."

It was true. The twin curves of the smooth nut were separated by a central cleft that made it look exactly like a curvy woman's derriere.

"You should see the other side," she said.

"It's not the same?"

She shook her head.

Max dropped the banana leaves and rolled the nut over, and despite knowing what to expect, Caro still felt a blush rise on her cheeks. The reverse looked just like her own rounded belly and thighs, complete with the triangle-shaped juncture where Max had touched her to such devastating effect.

Avoiding his eye, she adopted her most scholarly tones. "Because of its ... er ..."

"Erotic shape?"

"*Unusual appearance*, the coco de mer is thought to have mythological, even magical properties."

Max grunted. "I can see why. It's quite something."

"Legend has it that the trees make passionate love on stormy nights. They say the male trees uproot themselves and approach the female trees, and because they're so shy and secretive, anyone who sees them mating will either die, or go blind."

"Well, that's comforting." Max said. "Let's hope this one floated here from somewhere else. Even so, I'll keep my eyes closed, next time there's a storm. Wouldn't want to be an accidental voyeur."

Caro chuckled. Max's relaxed attitude made it impossible for her to be awkward about what they'd done together. She supposed she ought to be feeling ashamed for having allowed him such liberties, but she couldn't seem to dredge up an ounce of regret.

He insisted on carrying the nut back to camp, so Caro gathered the banana leaves and used them to improve the roof of their shelter. As the sun became hotter, she rested in the shade, half hoping Max would find an excuse to join her, but he took off around the headland, so she entertained herself by weaving palm fronds together to make a rudimentary sunhat.

If only she could read Max's thoughts. Was he thinking of her? If he truly believed himself a down-on-his-luck stable hand, might he be feeling guilty for giving in to her seduction?

Or was she just one more woman in a long line of conquests?

She'd remember the feel of his bare chest pressing her down, the wicked play of his fingers, for as long as she lived, but perhaps men were different. He could well have already dismissed the entire incident from his mind. She wasn't his first lover, after all.

Her heart gave a miserable little squeeze.

The heat was as draining and oppressive as her thoughts. She lay in the shelter and must have dozed, because when she awoke the sun was much lower in the sky and there was no sign of Max anywhere.

A flash of alarm caught her. He'd been gone for *hours*. What if he'd had an accident?

He wasn't on the adjacent beach, so she stacked more wood on the signal fire and waved half-heartedly over at the other island. She was just debating whether to carry on when she heard a whistle and looked up to see him appear over the promontory of rocks at the far end of the beach.

Her heart soared in relief. She might have wished to be alone when they'd first been washed ashore, but now she couldn't imagine not having his companionship.

For one foolish moment she wondered what it would be like if they were *never* rescued.

She could be happy, here, with him.

A rogue wave splashed her feet and she let out a soft snort at her own idiocy. This situation wasn't permanent. They would be rescued, eventually, and reality would intrude like a bucket of cold water to the face. Max would regain his memory, and they would each go their separate ways.

If she was truly unmarriageable when they reached London, she would remain a spinster, traveling the world and assisting her parents in their scientific endeavors. Max wouldn't consider her as his potential duchess. She was too unconventional, too unusual. And staying in England to watch him marry someone else would hurt.

"I thought you'd come to grief," she scolded when he was close enough to hear. "What will I do if you break your leg or get bitten by a shark?"

His teeth flashed in his tanned face. "I expect you'll put me out of my misery and finish me off with the pocket knife."

She shuddered at his morbid sense of humor. "Don't say that!"

"Oh, so you'd nurse me back to health?"

"I'd certainly *try*."

He snorted. "Only because it's too hot to dig me a grave. I heard what you said that first morning. You called me an insufferable oaf."

Caro turned her face away to hide her blush.

"I'm hoping your opinion of me has improved?" he pressed.

She started back toward camp, but he kept pace beside her easily, with his longer stride.

"Marginally," she conceded.

She caught his grin from the corner of her eye and felt an answering smile tug her own lips.

"Well, that's a relief. I won't be afraid of sharpening the blade."

"Perhaps you can use it to shave?"

He drew his fingers over his cheek and chin. "You don't like my stubble?"

Caro clenched her hands against the desire to stroke his cheek. "You look like a pirate."

His smile widened. "That's not an answer."

She lifted her nose in the air and ignored his taunting. The man's opinion of himself was high enough already. There was no need to admit she found him devastatingly attractive.

To cool off, she waded out into the shallows, lifting her skirts above her knees. Max started to clamber over the rocks, but she hadn't gone far when something brushed her calf and a stinging sensation prickled her skin.

She glanced down, and saw the clear dome and gently waving tentacles of a jellyfish, bobbing in the waves.

CHAPTER 16

"Oww! Jellyfish!"

Caro splashed ashore and bent to inspect her leg. The burning sensation had increased to pain, and even as she watched, a series of thin red stripes like rope burns appeared on her skin.

Max raced to her side and threw his arm around her shoulder, supporting her as she sank onto the sand. "Hold still."

"It really stings!" Caro bit her lip as a wave of light-headedness threatened.

"You're white as a sheet. Damn it."

"I'm feeling a little—"

"Hold on." He caught her under the knees and lifted her. Caro put her arms around his neck and held on, praying she wouldn't faint.

Her leg hurt like the devil, and she pressed her face into his chest and inhaled deeply. The wonderful musky scent of him filled her nose, and the racing of her heart slowed a little.

Back at camp he deposited her gently on the palm leaves she'd spread in front of the shelter, then rushed to fill one of the coconut bowls with fresh water.

"Here, drink this."

She sent him a wobbly smile of thanks.

A line of pale welts, like a beaded necklace, had now appeared within the red lesions on her leg. Max winced when he saw them, and he looked so worried that Caro felt the bizarre need to reassure him.

"It's not so bad," she said. "It just feels like I've been stung by a hundred stinging nettles."

He raked his hand through his hair. "God, if this was a musket wound, I'd know what to do, but I've never treated a jellyfish sting before. Any ideas?"

Caro took another sip of water and stretched out her leg. "Father was stung once, in Spain. I think they poured vinegar on it." She frowned. "Or maybe be it was wine? I was only ten, I can't remember."

"Well, we don't have either of those," Max growled. "Damn it."

"I seem to remember they also tried hot water."

"Now that I *can* do. Lie down."

Caro lay back weakly and watched as Max filled another of the coconut shells and nestled it among the glowing embers.

"Hold on, brave girl. It will take a while to heat." He bent to brush her hair back from her forehead. Caro closed her eyes and tried to concentrate on anything except the searing pain in her leg.

She heard Max moving around, and then felt the gentle brush of his hand on her arm. "Caro, sweetheart. The water's ready."

Max's unexpected endearment made her open her eyes. She found him leaning over her, the shocking blue of his stare unexpectedly close.

He sent her another of his heart-stopping smiles and his knuckles brushed her cheek. "Come on, soldier, sit up."

He'd folded his cravat into a makeshift pad, and she bit back an unladylike curse when he dipped it into the warm water and pressed it to the sting. Eventually, however, the pain subsided, and she sent him a relieved smile.

"It's working. It's not so bad now."

He let out an audible huff. "Thank God. It's too hot to dig you a grave."

Caro chuckled.

"I expect it'll hurt for a while, though" he continued. "Still, you can consider this just one more exotic injury to add to your tally. Was it worse than being bitten by a tarantula?"

"Definitely."

He shook his head. "You are a remarkable woman, Caro Montgomery. I've seen soldiers with a tiny splinter make more fuss than you. I swear, some of them cried for their mothers if they even grazed a knuckle."

Caro's cheeks heated at his compliment.

He rose to his feet. "Now, you stay right there while I go and get us some dinner."

True to his word, he managed to chase two silver-blue fish into her rock pool, and by the time the sun began to set the delicious scent of grilled fish made Caro's stomach rumble in anticipation.

The throbbing in her leg had almost completely subsided, so she hobbled over to the 'table' and sliced up the mangos and bananas. They ate the fish with their fingers from banana leaves, and Caro decided she'd never tasted anything so good in her life.

"Well, what a day."

Max leaned back against one of the palm trees with one knee bent, as relaxed as Caro had ever seen him. She tried to recall him back in England, perfectly attired and stiffly polite in some society ballroom, and failed.

"This is certainly the strangest Christmas day I've ever spent," she agreed.

A gust of wind fanned the fire and ruffled her hair and she

sighed, grateful for the breeze, but Max frowned over at the horizon.

"I don't like the look of those clouds. We're in for another storm."

She followed the direction of his gaze. It was almost dark, but she could just make out a bank of purple clouds rolling toward them. As if to confirm his theory a jagged bolt of lightning flickered along the underside of the dark mass, briefly illuminating it.

"One. Two." Caro began counting aloud to estimate how far away the storm was. Father had always taught her that one second equaled one mile, if one counted from the flash of lightning to the corresponding sound of thunder.

"Eleven. Twelve—" An ominous rumble boomed across the sea, as if a brewer was rolling heavy barrels of ale across a flagstone floor above them.

Max rose to his feet, filled with new purpose. "I'll secure the roof of the shelter. If the wind gets up, we don't want it blowing away. Or falling in on us."

"Would it be better to go inland? What if the waves come up this far?"

"I think we should be safe here. We're above the highest tide line, after all. And the reef should protect us from the worst of the waves. I'd rather stay here where it's more open than risk getting hit in the head by a falling branch or stray coconut."

The light was fading fast, and Max hurried to collect more strips of vine to secure the roof. Caro gathered extra firewood and stacked it under a pile of palm leaves to stay dry, then built up the fire into an impressive blaze.

She wondered if those on the other island would be able to see the glow of it over the headland, and prayed that they would be safe from the oncoming storm, too.

The flashes of lightning were almost constant now, and definitely closer. The thunder reverberated through her chest, but by the time the first raindrops spattered onto the fire they were as well-prepared as they could be.

Caro ducked under the leaves and shouted at Max over the rising wind.

"Come inside. You'll get drenched!"

He heeded her command, and she shuffled sideways to give him room. The open front of the shelter was high enough for them to sit up, and she pulled her knees to her chest as the rain began to come down in earnest.

Beside her, Max crossed his legs, tailor fashion, and the two of them watched as the fire leaped and sizzled in protest and the glowing red embers swirled in the wind. The surface of the lagoon danced with the downpour.

"Do you think the fire will withstand the storm?" She had to lean closer to Max to be heard over the steady drumming of the rain.

"I hope so," he answered, his lips close to her ear. "But I wouldn't bank on it."

A flash of lightning split the sky directly overhead followed by an ear-splitting crackle of thunder, and Caro let out an instinctive shriek that turned into a peal of laughter at her own foolishness.

"I've always loved storms," she shouted. "They make me feel funny—sort of tingly and excited and nervous at the same time. I can *feel* it, right here." She pressed her palm to her chest.

Max's answering amusement was clearly illuminated by the flickering red firelight. "Me, too. The power of nature is amazing, isn't it?"

His laughing gaze dropped to her hand, still pressed between her breasts, and Caro's pulse leapt in sudden awareness of their proximity. His shoulder was mere inches from her own, his knee pressing her leg, and the curtain of rain seemed to enclose them in their own private world.

"Just think," his lips lifted in a wicked smile, "Somewhere, out there, far from prying eyes, the coco de mer trees are uprooting themselves and making mad, passionate love."

His eyes flicked back to hers and held, and Caro's heart gave another jolt. Quick as lightning, her body was hot with desire, tingling with anticipation.

She licked her suddenly-dry lips. "I can't say I blame them. I mean, what else is there to do in weather like this?"

His gaze sharpened with a look that had her stomach clenching with excitement.

"Nothing," he murmured. "There's really nothing else to do."

"Except sleep," she said, perversely determined to tease him. "We could always try to sleep."

His dark brows rose. "Do you *want* to sleep Caro?"

CHAPTER 17

Caro could barely breathe. She knew what he was asking, what she desired. If she was a good girl, a dutiful girl, a girl who followed the rules, she would tell him yes, she wanted to sleep.

But the wildness of the storm had stirred up an answering wildness inside her. Something deep and yearning and primitive. She wanted his strong arms around her, his big body on hers. She wanted the same passion and intensity as the lightning, the thunder, the rain.

She might not have this man forever. But she had him here, now. Life was precarious at best. She could have drowned the night of the storm. And what if she'd stepped on a deadly lionfish today, instead of a relatively innocuous jellyfish? She would have been dead by now. She'd be a fool not to seize her chance.

Decision made, she lifted her hand and traced her fingers across his lips, then trailed them along his prickly jaw. His eyes flared and he opened his mouth to say something, but she didn't let him speak.

"No, Max. I don't want to sleep."

Caro held her breath. The incessant pounding of the rain matched the roar of her own pulse in her ears.

For a heartbeat Max sat frozen, and she wondered if he'd turn her down, but then his hand shot out to cup her nape and he tugged her forward for a kiss as intense as the storm outside.

His lips played over hers again and again, increasing her desire to a fever pitch, and a wicked, throbbing ache pulsed between her thighs. She pressed herself against him, stroking his hair, his shoulders.

"Please, make love to me."

He pulled back, just a fraction. "Caro. Are you sure?"

She nodded, then realized he probably couldn't see her; the fire was almost completely out, vanquished by the relentless deluge.

"Yes," she said. "I'm sure."

"I can make certain you don't get with child," he said gruffly. His voice was a low rasp, as if speaking was an effort. "I can pull out, before I finish."

She cupped his jaw. "I trust you. Yes. Please."

Max groaned, and then his lips claimed hers, melding them together into one being. Caro leaned into him, but when he tried to take her in his arms his shoulder hit the wooden frame and the whole shelter shook alarmingly.

"Damn it, I wish we were in a bed," he growled.

Caro smiled into the darkness. "Should we lie down?"

"That's an excellent idea."

He pulled away from her and she stretched out, stifling a laugh at the sound of his frantic movements as he tried to shed his shirt and wriggle out of his breeches in the enclosed space. Several muffled expletives echoed from his side as she pulled her own dress up over her head, but her amusement fled as he rolled back toward her and found her mouth again.

He half-covered her with his body and the incredible heat of him seeped through the cotton of her shift. His palm slid up the outside of her thigh, rough and urgent against her skin, and she writhed against him, desperate for more.

He obliged. Her senses swam as his hair-roughened leg slid between hers and she groaned into his mouth. And when his hand moved to her breast, squeezing and fondling, she cried out her pleasure.

Lightning crackled overhead, briefly illuminating his chest and arms as he held himself over her, then they were plunged into darkness once more. His breath was hot as he kissed his way down the side of her throat, interspersing his kisses with mumbled terms of encouragement.

"God, Caro, yes. That's right. Touch me."

She ran her fingers through his hair, then did some exploring of her own; tracing the curves of his shoulders, the muscles that bracketed his spine. Beyond shame, she dug her nails into his curved buttocks and received a groan of encouragement against her breast as he teethed the stiff nipple through the fabric.

Waves crashed on the shore, but Caro could barely hear them over the pounding of her own heartbeat. Max was everywhere, all around her, his taste, his scent.

He moved fully over her, supporting himself with bent elbows on either side of her head. His flat stomach pressed hers and the hard shaft of his manhood notched in the lee of her spread legs.

Caro tensed as he slid his hand between them and touched her, as he'd done at the waterfall. Her breath was coming in excited pants, but she arched up wordlessly into him, silently begging for more of that glorious pleasure he'd shown her before.

He didn't disappoint. His wicked fingers swirled and teased, driving her higher before leaving her cruelly unsatisfied. But her groan of complaint died on her lips as he reached down and positioned the head of his cock to her slippery entrance.

They both stilled.

"You're sure?" he breathed against her lips. "Last chance to say no."

She lifted up and pressed her mouth to his. "Do it, Cavendish, or I'll stab you with that stupid knife of yours."

His chuckle morphed into a low growl of pleasure as he pressed his hips forward and slowly, slowly entered her.

Caro opened her eyes wide in the darkness, absorbing this astonishing new sensation with a sense of awe. He pulled out a little, then he slid back inside, even further this time, and a shimmer of dark delight raced along her limbs.

"That's it," he whispered against her temple. "Let me in. Let me love you, Caro."

He pressed further, stretching her, but her body yielded to his invasion. He rocked back and forth in a maddening rhythm that made her catch her breath and arch up, straining for more of the delicious friction.

She gripped his hair, urging him on, as tension built in her muscles, clamoring for release. His movements rubbed a spot deep inside that built and built until suddenly, with a cry of elation, her entire body flew apart.

Lightning flashed behind her closed eyelids as pleasure pulsed through her body. Max wasn't far behind. With a groan that seemed dragged from the center of his chest, he thrust once more inside her then withdrew from her body. He pressed himself, full weight, upon her and Caro felt the hot tide of his release against her stomach.

For a brief moment they lay completely still, hearts hammering in tandem. And then Max rolled off her with a sound that was half groan, half exhausted chuckle.

"Dear God, I knew you'd be the end of me, Montgomery."

Caro tried hard to catch her breath. Her entire body was glowing, replete with a wonderful lethargy.

"Well, if it's any consolation, you've killed me too," she managed weakly.

He cleaned them both off with his discarded cravat, then shifted back to her. Silently, he rolled her so that she was facing away from him, then threw his arm over her waist and tugged her backward, nestling her bottom into the curve of his groin, surrounding her with his body.

Caro had no objections. Their exertions had brought a sheen of sweat to her skin, but now she was cooling off. A gust of wind battered the shelter and she shivered involuntarily.

"Cold?" Max's voice was muffled as he pressed his mouth to her neck.

"A little."

His arm tightened, drawing her closer into the shelter of his body, and she let out a little sigh of contentment.

"Don't worry. I'll keep you warm."

CHAPTER 18

Caro awoke at dawn, still in Max's arms. She must have turned over in the night, because now the top of her head was tucked under his chin and her flattened hand rested on his glorious chest. His left arm was thrown over her waist, and his heart beat, sure and steady, thumped beneath her palm.

"Ah, awake at last."

Max's voice, deep and gravelly with sleep, rumbled above her, and she pulled back to look up into his face.

Despite her resolution to be mature and sophisticated, the feel of his body pressed so intimately to hers made heat rise to her cheeks.

The storm had passed. The rising sun warmed the angles of his cheeks and gilded the straight line of his nose, and Caro's heart gave a little squeeze inside her chest.

Oh, she was going to miss him.

She tried to memorize every detail, to burn it into her memory so that when she was back in cold, rainy old England she would be able to remember the sheer heaven of being held like this, in his arms.

"Still deciding whether to stab me?" Max's blue eyes twinkled at her. "Because I distinctly remember you threatening me with such a thing last night."

"Only if you didn't make love to me."

"Which I did." He narrowed his eyes at her. "Was it not satisfactory?"

"Oh, it was *very* satisfactory. As well you know, you scoundrel."

"Glad to hear it. Wouldn't want the woman I plan to marry dissatisfied with my performance."

Caro stilled, gazing up at him in shock. "Wait. Marry? What?"

Max smoothed a strand of hair from her cheek and stared deep into her eyes. "I'd like to marry you, Caroline Montgomery. If you'll have me, of course."

Her heart began to pound. "You don't mean that. You don't know what you're saying. You don't even know who you are. I mean—"

"You don't want to marry a stable hand?"

"It's not that. It's just that . . . you don't have to marry me just because we've—you know—"

She waved her hand vaguely between them, horribly aware that she was babbling.

Oh, this was both the best and worst day of her life. She'd never imagined she'd receive a proposal of marriage from Max, and while there was nothing she wanted more than to be his wife, how could she say yes, when he had no idea who he was?

To accept would be to entrap him in the worst possible way. As a gentleman, he'd be too honorable to withdraw his offer, once he learned he was a duke. He'd regret it, and come to resent her in the process.

"Cavorted?" he supplied. "Made love?"

"Because I'm ruined," she managed. "There's no need. Honestly. I don't care what the gossips will say back in London. Please don't feel like you have to offer just to save my reputation."

Max's laugh cut off her protests. He pressed a kiss to her forehead and pulled back, shaking his head.

"Oh, Caro. That's not why I want you to marry me. I love you. I want you beside me. Forever."

"You're not a groom," she blurted out desperately. "I lied. You're not penniless either. Your uncle left you an enormous house and a huge pile of money and you're—"

"The Duke of Hayworth?" He grinned down at her, his blue eyes twinkling with devilry.

Caro was certain her heart actually stopped.

"You remember?" she croaked.

"Never forgot."

She scowled up at him in dawning horror, then whacked him on the chest with her balled fist. "You know you're a duke?"

"Of course."

"How long have you known?"

He *laughed*, the beast.

"Since about five minutes after I opened my eyes on the beach that first day."

"Ohhh, you monster—"

"A groomsman?!" he chided. "Really? Was that the best you could do? Why not make me a chimney sweep or a tinker? Or one of those mudlarks, who wade about on the side of the Thames at low tide picking up rubbish?"

"I think I might stab you, after all," she growled.

He caught her wrists and restrained her with the lightest of holds.

"I love you," he repeated softly. "Of all the people in the world I could have wished to be shipwrecked with, I'd always and forever choose you."

Caro could barely think. Happiness was constricting her chest, but she was afraid to believe that this was real, and not a cruel dream.

"But I love *you*," she said, almost accusingly. "I think I always have."

He released her wrists and slid his fingers between hers so their hands were entwined.

"Is that a yes? You'll be my duchess? Just think, if we can get along under trying conditions like this, we'll have no problem living together in my London town house, or at Gatcombe Park."

He slanted her a hungry, heated look that made her pulse race. "I want to make love to you in a bathtub filled with rose petals, in a huge soft feather bed piled high with cushions—"

Caro groaned. "Ohh, you beast. Don't tempt me. What if we're never rescued?"

"Then I'll be perfectly happy making love to you right here, in this awful, uncomfortable hut, for the rest of my days. We'll be the duke and duchess of Heaven-Knows-Where." Max's hands cupped her cheeks as he tilted her face up to his. "Say yes, Caro."

The sun burst over the horizon, flooding them both with light, and Caro pressed her lips to his. "In that case, Maximillian Cavendish, yes. I'll marry you."

CHAPTER 19

On the thirty first day of December, New Year's Eve, Caro glanced up from her hibiscus flower tea and saw a tall plume of smoke rising over the headland.

"Max! The other island's signal fire!"

Max, who had been dozing in the shelter after a night of lovemaking that made Caro blush to recall it—*who knew a man could do such wicked, exquisite things with his tongue, for heaven's sake?*—leapt to his feet.

"Quick!"

He snatched a stick from the fire, and together they raced along the beach and clambered onto the rocks.

Sure enough, a fire blazed on the opposite beach, and Caro gave a whoop of sheer elation as she spied a ship with billowing white sails heading toward the strait.

"We're saved!"

Max caught her in an impulsive hug, then leaped down and put the glowing torch to the tinder beneath their own signal fire. Since they'd been diligently keeping it ready, it caught almost immediately, and Caro heaped handfuls of damp leaves onto it to make it smoke.

As the ship drew closer, they could see crew members moving about on the deck, and Max squinted to make out the flag that fluttered from the rigging.

"It's a Royal Naval ship," he grinned. "I wonder how they found us."

"Who cares!" Caro laughed, giddy with relief. "We're going back to hot baths and soft beds and food that isn't mango. I never want to eat another mango ever again."

Max kissed the top of her head. "Very well. If that's your wish." He smiled down at her. "Would you like to be married at St. George's, Hanover Square?"

Caro wrinkled her nose. "I don't mind. Wherever you want."

"Because I was thinking..."

"What?"

"What if we present everyone with a fait accompli and get married before we get back to London? The ship's captain can marry us. We could do it here, before we set sail."

Caro went up on tiptoe and pressed a kiss to his cheek. "Oh, yes, I love that idea! My clothes should still be on the *Artemis*. We can marry on the deck, in front of my family."

"I'll have to formally ask your father permission to court you."

Caro snorted. "It's a little late for that. And besides, they've always liked you. I can't imagine they'll be disappointed that you're joining the family. You're not a *Davies,* after all."

* * *

CAROLINE MONTGOMERY AND MAXIMILLIAN CAVENDISH, his Grace, the fourteenth Duke of Hayworth, were married at sunset on the deck of *HMS Carron*. The bride's immediate family were in attendance, and the bride carried a bouquet of tropical blooms.

As the sky turned an extravagant array of pinks and reds, Max joined Caro at the ship's rail and they both gazed back at the tiny island that had been their home for the past ten eventful days.

Caro leaned her head against her new husband's shoulder. "This might sound strange, but I'm going to miss this place. Despite all the hardships, we had some truly memorable moments. I'm glad we were stranded. Together. Alone."

Max put his arm around her waist and pulled her into his side. "Me too."

"I can't believe you insisted on bringing the coco de mer home, though."

"And why not? We might be the only couple in England to have one. And how could I leave it behind? It has such fond memories attached to it."

"As do thunderstorms," she added, blushing.

He chuckled. "Plenty of those in England, too."

Caro shook her head. "We might have missed Christmas, but we'll be home in time for the twins to make their debut in society. I wonder what they'll make of the *Ton*."

Max gave her a loving squeeze. "The real question is, what will the *Ton* make of the twins? They're going to cause chaos, I guarantee."

"At least they'll have an older sister who's a duchess."

"A *scandalous* duchess." Max turned her in his arms. "A desert island duchess."

Caro glanced over her shoulder and was relieved to find the remaining crew members had all discreetly found engrossing things to do elsewhere. She lifted her face for a kiss.

"Well, if I'm a desert island duchess, then that makes you my desert island duke," she smiled. "I hope this won't be our last adventure together, Your Grace."

Max kissed her soundly. "It won't be. I have a feeling our adventures are only just beginning, my love."

THE END

Love what you just read? Read on for a sneak peek of *This Earl Of Mine,*
the first exhilarating historical romance in Kate Bateman's Bow Street Bachelors Series...

Find more of Kate's books here on her website: www.kcbateman.com

THIS EARL OF MINE

London, March 1816.

THERE WERE WORSE PLACES to find a husband than Newgate Prison.

Of course there were.

It was just that, at present, Georgie couldn't think of any.

"Georgiana Caversteed, this is a terrible idea."

Georgie frowned at her burly companion, Pieter Smit, as the nondescript carriage he'd summoned to convey them to London's most notorious jail rocked to a halt on the cobbled street. The salt-weathered Dutchman always used her full name whenever he disapproved of something she was doing. Which was often.

"Your father would turn in his watery grave if he knew what you were about."

That was undoubtedly true. Until three days ago, enlisting a husband from amongst the ranks of London's most dangerous criminals had not featured prominently on her list of life goals.

But desperate times called for desperate measures. Or, in this case, for a desperate felon about to be hanged. A felon she would marry before the night was through.

Georgie peered out into the rain-drizzled street, then up, up the near-windowless walls. They rose into the mist, five stories high, a vast expanse of brickwork, bleak and unpromising. A church bell tolled somewhere in the darkness, a forlorn clang like a death knell. Her stomach knotted with a grim sense of foreboding.

Was she really going to go through with this? It had seemed a good plan, in the safety of Grosvenor Square. The perfect way to thwart Cousin Josiah once and for all. She stepped from the carriage, ducked her head against the rain, and followed Pieter under a vast arched gate. Her heart hammered at the audacity of what she planned.

They'd taken the same route as condemned prisoners on the way to Tyburn tree, only in reverse. West to east, from the rarefied social strata of Mayfair through gradually rougher and bleaker neighborhoods, Holborn and St. Giles, to this miserable place where the dregs of humanity had been incarcerated. Georgie felt as if she were nearing her own execution.

She shook off the pervasive aura of doom and straightened her spine. This was her choice. However unpalatable the next few minutes might be, the alternative was far worse. Better a temporary marriage to a murderous, unwashed criminal than a lifetime of misery with Josiah.

They crossed the deserted outer courtyard, and Georgie cleared her throat, trying not to inhale the foul-smelling air that seeped from the very pores of the building. "You have it all arranged? They are expecting us?"

Pieter nodded. "Aye. I've greased the wheels with yer blunt, my girl. The proctor and the ordinary are both bent as copper shillings. Used to having their palms greased, those two, the greedy bastards."

Her father's right-hand man had never minced words in front of her, and Georgie appreciated his bluntness. So few people in the ton ever said what they really meant. Pieter's honesty was refreshing. He'd been her father's man for twenty years before she'd even been born. A case of mumps had prevented him from accompanying William Caversteed on his last, fateful voyage, and Georgie had often thought that if Pieter had been with her father, maybe he'd still be alive. Little things like squalls, shipwrecks, and attacks from Barbary pirates would be mere inconveniences to a man like Pieter Smit.

In the five years since Papa's death, Pieter's steadfast loyalty had been dedicated to William's daughters, and Georgie loved the gruff, hulking manservant like a second father. He would see her through this madcap scheme—even if he disapproved.

She tugged the hood of her cloak down to stave off the drizzle. This place was filled with murderers, highwaymen, forgers, and thieves. Poor wretches slated to die, or those "lucky" few whose sentences had been commuted to transportation. Yet in her own way, she was equally desperate.

"You are sure that this man is to be hanged tomorrow?"

Pieter nodded grimly as he rapped on a wooden door. "I am. A low sort he is, by all accounts."

She shouldn't ask, didn't want to know too much about the man whose name she was purchasing. A man whose death would spell her own freedom. She would be wed and widowed within twenty-four hours.

Taking advantage of a condemned man left a sour taste in her mouth, a sense of guilt that her happiness should come from the misfortune of another. But this man would die whether she married him or not. "What are his crimes?"

"Numerous, I'm told. He's a coiner." At her frown, Pieter elaborated. "Someone who forges coins. It's treason, that."

"Oh." That seemed a little harsh. She couldn't imagine what that was like, having no money, forced to make your own. Still, having a fortune was almost as much of a curse as having nothing. She'd endured six years of insincere, lecherous fortune hunters, thanks to her bountiful coffers.

"A smuggler too," Pieter added for good measure. "Stabbed a customs man down in Kent."

She was simply making the best out of a bad situation. This man would surely realize that while there was no hope for himself, at least he could leave this world having provided for whatever family he left behind. Everyone had parents, or siblings, or lovers. Everyone had a price. She, of all people, knew that—she was buying herself a husband. At least this way there was no pretense. Besides, what was the point in having a fortune if you couldn't use it to make yourself happy?

Pieter hammered impatiently on the door again.

"I know you disapprove," Georgie muttered. "But Father would never have wanted me to marry a man who covets my purse more than my person. If you hadn't rescued me the other evening, that's precisely what would have happened. I would have had to wed Josiah to prevent a scandal. I refuse to give control of my life and my fortune to some idiot to mismanage. As a widow, I will be free."

Pieter gave an eloquent sniff.

"You think me heartless," Georgie said. "But can you think of another way?" At his frowning silence, she nodded. "No, me neither."

Heavy footsteps and the jangle of keys finally heralded proof of human life inside. The door scraped open, and the low glare of a lantern illuminated a grotesquely large man in the doorway.

"Mr. Knollys?"

The man gave a brown-toothed grin as he recognized Pieter. "Welcome back, sir. Welcome back." He craned his neck and raised the lantern, trying to catch a glimpse of Georgie. "You brought the lady, then?" His piggy eyes narrowed with curiosity within the folds of his flabby face.

"And the license." Pieter tapped the pocket of his coat.

Knollys nodded and stepped back, allowing them entry. "The ordinary's agreed to perform the service." He turned and began shuffling down the narrow corridor, lantern raised. "Only one small problem." He cocked his head back toward Pieter. "That cove the lady was to marry? Cheated the 'angman, 'e 'as."

Pieter stopped abruptly, and Georgie bumped into his broad back.

"He's dead?" Pieter exclaimed. "Then why are we here? You can damn well return that purse I paid you!"

The man's belly undulated grotesquely as he laughed. It was not a kindly sound. "Now, now. Don't you worry yerself none, me fine lad. That special license don't have no names on it yet, do it? No. We've plenty more like 'im in this place. This way."

The foul stench of the prison increased tenfold as they followed the unpleasant Knollys up some stairs and down a second corridor. Rows of thick wooden doors, each with a square metal hatch and a sliding shutter at eye level lined the walls on either side. Noises emanated from some—inhuman moans, shouts, and foul curses. Others were ominously silent. Georgie pressed her handkerchief to her nose, glad she'd doused it in lavender water.

Knollys waddled to a stop in front of the final door in the row. His eyes glistened with a disquieting amount of glee.

"Found the lady a substitute, I 'ave." He thumped the metal grate with his meaty fist and eyed Georgie's cloaked form with a knowing, suggestive leer that made her feel as though she'd been drenched in cooking fat. She resisted the urge to shudder.

"Wake up, lads!" he bellowed. "There's a lady 'ere needs yer services."

Chapter 2.

BENEDICT WILLIAM HENRY WYLDE, scapegrace second son of the late Earl of Morcott, reluctant war hero, and former scourge of the ton, strained to hear the last words of his cellmate. He bent forward, trying to ignore the stench of the man's blackened teeth and the sickly sweet scent of impending death that wreathed his feverish form.

Silas had been sick for days, courtesy of a festering stab wound in his thigh. The bastard jailers hadn't heeded his pleas for water, bandages, or laudanum. Ben had been trying to decipher the smuggler's ranting for hours. Delirium had loosened the man's tongue, and he'd leaned close, waiting for something useful to slip between those cracked lips, but the words had been frustratingly fragmented. Silas raved about plots and treasons. An Irishman. The emperor. Benedict had been on the verge of shaking the poor bastard when his crewmate let out one last, gasping breath—and died.

"Oh, bloody hell!"

Ben drew back from the hard, straw-filled pallet that stank of piss and death. He'd been so close to getting the information he needed.

Not for the first time, he cursed his friend Alex's uncle, Sir Nathaniel Conant, Chief Magistrate of Bow Street and the man tasked with transforming the way London was policed. Bow Street was the senior magistrate court in the capital, and the "Runners," as they were rather contemptuously known, investigated crimes, followed up leads, served warrants and summons, searched properties for stolen goods, and watched premises where infringements of bylaws or other offences were suspected.

Conant had approached Ben, Alex, and their friend Seb about a year ago, a few months after their return from fighting Napoleon on the continent. The three of them had just opened the Tricorn Club—the gambling hell they'd pledged to run together while crouched around a smoky campfire in Belgium. Conant had pointed out that their new venture placed them in an ideal position for gathering intelligence on behalf of His Majesty's government, since its members—and their acquaintances—came from all levels of society. He'd also requested their assistance on occasional cases, especially those which bridged the social divide. The three of them not only had entrée into polite society, but thanks to their time in the Rifles, they dealt equally well with those from the lower end of the social spectrum, the "scum of the earth," as Wellington had famously called his own troops.

Conant paid the three of them a modest sum for every mission they undertook, plus extra commission for each bit of new information they brought in. Neither Alex nor Seb needed the money; they were more interested in the challenge to their wits, but Benedict had jumped at the chance of some additional income, even though the work was sometimes—such as now—less than glamorous.

He was in Newgate on Conant's orders, chasing a rumor that someone had been trying to assemble a crew of smugglers to rescue the deposed Emperor Napoleon from the island of St. Helena. Benedict had been ingratiating himself with this band for weeks, posing as a bitter ex-navy gunner, searching for the man behind such a plan. He'd even allowed himself to be seized by customs officials near Gravesend along with half the gang—recently deceased Silas amongst them—in the hopes of discovering more. If he solved this case, he'd receive a reward of five hundred pounds, which could go some way toward helping his brother pay off the mass of debt left by their profligate father.

He'd been in here almost ten days now. The gang's ringleader, a vicious bastard named Hammond, had been hanged yesterday morning. Ben, Silas, and two of the younger gang members had been sentenced to transportation. That was British leniency for you; a nice slow death on a prison ship instead of a quick drop from Tyburn tree.

The prison hulk would be leaving at dawn, but Ben wouldn't be on it. There was no need to hang around now that Silas and Hammond were both dead. He'd get nothing more from them. And the two youngsters, Peters and Fry, were barely in their teens. They knew nothing useful. Conant had arranged for him to "disappear" from the prison hulk before it sailed; its guards were as open to bribery as Knollys.

Several other gang members had escaped the Gravesend raid. Benedict had glimpsed a few familiar faces in the crowd when the magistrate had passed down his sentence. He'd have to chase them down as soon as he was free and see if any of them had been approached for the traitorous mission.

Benedict sighed and slid down the wall until he sat on the filthy floor, his knees bent in front of him. He'd forgotten what it felt like to be clean. He rasped one hand over his stubbled jaw and grimaced—he'd let his beard grow out as a partial disguise. He'd commit murder for a wash and a razor. Even during the worst scrapes in the Peninsular War, and then in France and Belgium, he'd always found time to shave. Alex and Seb, his brothers-in-arms, had mocked him for it mercilessly.

He glanced at the square of rain visible through the tiny barred grate on the outer wall of his cell. Seb and Alex were out there, lucky buggers, playing merry hell with the debutantes, wives, and widows of London with amazing impartiality.

The things he did for king and bloody country.

And cash, of course. Five hundred pounds was nothing to sneeze at.

Tracking down a traitor was admirable. Having to stay celibate and sober because there was neither a woman nor grog to be had in prison was hell. What he wouldn't give for some decent French brandy and a warm, willing wench. Hell, right now he'd settle for some of that watered-down ratafia they served at society balls and a tumble with a barmaid.

A pretty barmaid, of course. His face had always allowed him to be choosy. At least, it did when he was clean-shaven. His own mother probably wouldn't recognize him right now.

Voices and footsteps intruded on his errant fancies as the obsequious voice of Knollys echoed through the stones. A fist slammed into the grate, loud enough to wake the dead, and Benedict glanced over at Silas with morbid humor. Well, almost loud enough.

"Wake up, lads!" Knollys bellowed. "There's a lady 'ere needs yer services."

Benedict's brows rose in the darkness. What the devil?

"Ye promised ten pounds if I'd find 'er a man an' never say nuffink to nobody," he heard Knollys say through the door.

"Are they waiting to hang too?" An older man's voice, that, with a foreign inflexion. Dutch, perhaps.

"Nay. Ain't got no more for the gallows. Not since Hammond yesterday." Knollys sounded almost apologetic. "But either one of these'll fit the bill. Off to Van Diemen's Land they are, at first light."

"No, that won't do at all."

Benedict's ears pricked up at the sound of the cultured female voice. She sounded extremely peeved.

"I specifically wanted a condemned man, Mr. Knollys."

"Better come back in a week or so then, milady."

There was a short pause as the two visitors apparently conferred, too low for him to hear.

"I cannot wait another few weeks." The woman sounded resigned. "Very well. Let's see what you have."

Keys grated in the lock and Knollys's quivering belly filled the doorway. Benedict shielded his eyes from the lantern's glare, blinding after the semidarkness of the cell. The glow illuminated Silas's still figure on the bed and Knollys grunted.

"Dead, is 'e?" He sounded neither dismayed nor surprised. "Figured he wouldn't last the week. You'll 'ave to do then, Wylde. Get up."

Benedict pushed himself to his feet with a wince.

"Ain't married, are you, Wylde?" Knollys muttered, low enough not to be heard by those in the corridor.

"Never met the right woman," Benedict drawled, being careful to retain the rough accent of an east coast smuggler he'd adopted. "Still, one lives in 'ope."

Knollys frowned, trying to decide whether Ben was being sarcastic. As usual, he got it wrong. "This lady's 'ere to wed," he grunted finally, gesturing vaguely behind him.

Benedict squinted. Two shapes hovered just outside, partly shielded by the jailer's immense bulk. One of them, the smaller hooded figure, might possibly be female. "What woman comes here to marry?"

Knollys chuckled. "A desperate one, Mr. Wylde."

The avaricious glint in Knollys's eye hinted that he saw the opportunity to take advantage, and Benedict experienced a rush of both anger and protectiveness for the foolish woman, whoever she might be. Probably one of the muslin set, seeking a name for her unborn child. Or some common trollop, hoping her debts would be wiped off with the death of her husband. Except he'd never met a tart who spoke with such a clipped, aristocratic accent.

"You want me to marry some woman I've never met?" Benedict almost laughed in disbelief. "I appreciate the offer, Mr. Knollys, but I'll have to decline. I ain't stepping into the parson's mousetrap for no one."

Knollys took a menacing step forward. "Oh, you'll do it, Wylde, or I'll have Ennis bash your skull in." He glanced over at Silas's corpse. "I can just as easy 'ave 'im dig two graves instead of one."

Ennis was a short, troll-like thug who possessed fewer brains than a sack of potatoes, but he took a malicious and creative pleasure in administering beatings with his heavy wooden cudgel. Benedict's temper rose. He didn't like being threatened. If it weren't for the manacles binding his hands, he'd explain that pertinent fact to Mr. Knollys in no uncertain terms.

Unfortunately, Knollys wasn't a man to take chances. He prodded Benedict with his stick. "Out with ye. And no funny business." His meaty fist cuffed Ben around the head to underscore the point.

Benedict stepped out into the dim passageway and took an appreciative breath. The air was slightly less rancid out here. Of course, it was all a matter of degree.

A broad, grizzled man of around sixty moved to stand protectively in front of the woman, arms crossed and bushy brows lowered. Benedict leaned sideways and tried to make out her features, but the hood of a domino shielded her face. She made a delicious, feminine rustle of silk as she stepped back, though. No rough worsted and cotton for this lady. Interesting.

Knollys prodded him along the passage, and Benedict shook his head to dispel a sense of unreality. Here he was, unshaven, unwashed, less than six hours from freedom, and apparently about to be wed to a perfect stranger. It seemed like yet another cruel joke by fate.

He'd never imagined himself marrying. Not after the disastrous example of his own parents' union. His mother had endured his father's company only long enough to produce the requisite heir and a spare, then removed herself to the gaiety of London. For the next twenty years, she'd entertained a series of lovers in the town house, while his father had remained immured in Herefordshire with a succession of steadily younger live-in mistresses, one of whom had taken it upon herself to introduce a seventeen-year-old Benedict to the mysteries of the female form. It was a pattern of domesticity Benedict had absolutely no desire to repeat.

In truth, he hadn't thought he'd survive the war and live to the ripe old age of twenty-eight. If he had ever been forced to picture his own wedding—under torture, perhaps—he was fairly certain he wouldn't have imagined it taking place in prison. At the very least, he would have had his family and a couple of friends in attendance; his fellow sworn bachelors, Alex and Seb. Some flowers, maybe. A country church.

He'd never envisaged the lady. If three years of warfare had taught him anything, it was that life was too short to tie himself to one woman for the rest of his life. Marriage would be an imprisonment worse than his cell here in Newgate.

They clattered down the stairs and into the tiny chapel where the ordinary, Horace Cotton, was waiting, red-faced and unctuous. Cotton relished his role of resident chaplain; he enjoyed haranguing soon-to-be-dead prisoners with lengthy sermons full of fire and brimstone. No doubt he was being paid handsomely for this evening's work.

Benedict halted in front of the altar—little more than a table covered in a white cloth and two candles—and raised his manacled wrists to Knollys. The jailer sniffed but clearly realized he'd have to unchain him if they were to proceed. He gave Ben a sour, warning look as the irons slipped off, just daring him to try something. Ben shot him a cocky, challenging sneer in return.

How to put a stop to this farce? He had no cash to bribe his way out. A chronic lack of funds was precisely why he'd been working for Bow Street since his return from France, chasing thief-taker's rewards.

Could he write the wrong name on the register, to invalidate the marriage? Probably not. Both Knollys and Cotton knew him as Ben Wylde. Ex-Rifle brigade, penniless, cynical veteran of Waterloo. It wasn't his full name, of course, but it would probably be enough to satisfy the law.

Announcing that his brother happened to be the Earl of Morcott would certainly make matters interesting, but thanks to their father's profligacy, the estate was mortgaged to the hilt. John had even less money than Benedict.

The unpleasant sensation that he'd been neatly backed into a corner made Benedict's neck prickle, as if a French sniper had him in his sights. Still, he'd survived worse. He was a master at getting out of scrapes. Even if he was forced to marry this mystery harridan, there were always alternatives. An annulment, for one.

"Might I at least have the name of the lady to whom I'm about to be joined in holy matrimony?" he drawled.

The manservant scowled at the ironic edge to his tone, but the woman laid a silencing hand on his arm and stepped around him.

"You can indeed, sir." In one smooth movement, she pulled the hood from her head and faced him squarely. "My name is Georgiana Caversteed."

Benedict cursed in every language he knew.

Chapter 3.

GEORGIANA CAVERSTEED? What devil's trick was this?

He knew the name, but he'd never seen the face—until now. God's teeth, every man in London knew the name. The chit was so rich, she might as well have her own bank. She could have her pick of any man in England. What in God's name was she doing in Newgate looking for a husband?

Benedict barely remembered not to bow—an automatic response to being introduced to a lady of quality—and racked his brains to recall what he knew of her family. A cit's daughter. Her father had been in shipping, a merchant, rich as Croesus. He'd died and left the family a fortune.

The younger sister was said to be the beauty of the family, but she must indeed be goddess, because Georgiana Caversteed was strikingly lovely. Her arresting, heart-shaped face held a small straight nose and eyes which, in the candlelight, appeared to be dark grey, the color of wet slate. Her brows were full, her lashes long, and her mouth was soft and a fraction too wide.

A swift heat spread throughout his body, and his heart began to pound.

She regarded him steadily as he made his assessment, neither dipping her head nor coyly fluttering her lashes. Benedict's interest kicked up a notch at her directness, and a twitch in his breeches reminded him with unpleasantly bad timing of his enforced abstinence. This was neither the time nor the place to do anything about that.

They'd never met in the ton. She must have come to town after he'd left for the peninsula three years ago, which would make her around twenty-four. Most women would be considered on the shelf at that age, unmarried after so many social seasons, but with the near-irresistible lure of her fortune and with those dazzling looks, Georgiana Caversteed could be eighty-four and someone would still want her.

And yet here she was.

Benedict kept his expression bland, even as he tried to breathe normally. What on earth had made her take such drastic action? Was the chit daft in the head? He couldn't imagine any situation desperate enough to warrant getting leg-shackled to a man like him.

She moistened her lips with the tip of her tongue—which sent another shot of heat straight to his gut—and fixed him with an imperious glare. "What is your name, sir?" She took a step closer, almost in challenge, in defiance of his unchained hands and undoubtedly menacing demeanor.

He quelled a spurt of admiration for her courage, even if it was ill-advised. His inhaled breath caught a subtle whiff of her perfume. It made his knees weak. He'd forgotten the intoxicating scent of woman and skin. For one foolish moment, he imagined pulling her close and pressing his nose into her hair, just filling his lungs with the divine scent of her. He wanted to drink in her smell. He wanted to see if those lips really were as soft as they looked.

He took an involuntary step toward her but stopped at the low growl of warning from her manservant. Sanity prevailed, and he just remembered to stay in the role of rough smuggler they all expected of him.

"My name? Ben Wylde. At your service."

* * *

His voice was a deep rasp, rough from lack of use, and Georgie's stomach did an odd little flip. She needed to take command here, like Father on board one of his ships, but the man facing her was huge, hairy, and thoroughly intimidating.

When she'd glanced around Knollys's rotund form and into the gloomy cell, her first impression of the prisoner had been astonishment at his sheer size. He'd seemed to fill the entire space, all broad shoulders, wide chest, and long legs. She'd been expecting some poor, ragged, cowering scrap of humanity. Not this strapping, unapologetically male creature.

She'd studied his shaggy, overlong hair and splendid proportions from the back as they'd traipsed down the corridor. He stood a good head taller than Knollys, and unlike the jailer's waddling shuffle, this man walked with a long, confident stride, straight-backed and chin high, as if he owned the prison and were simply taking a tour for his pleasure.

Now, in the chapel, she finally saw his face—the parts that weren't covered with a dark bristle of beard—and her skin prickled as she allowed her eyes to rove over him. She pretended she was inspecting a horse or a piece of furniture. Something large and impersonal.

His dark hair was matted and hung around his face almost to his chin. It was hard to tell what color it would be when it was clean. A small wisp of straw stuck out from one side, just above his ear, and she resisted a bizarre feminine urge to reach up and remove it. Dark beard hid the shape of his jaw, but the candlelight caught his slanted cheekbones and cast shadows in the hollows beneath. The skin that she could see—a straight slash of nose, cheeks, and forehead—was unfashionably tanned and emphasized his deep brown eyes.

She'd stepped as close to him as she dared; no doubt he'd smell like a cesspool if she got any nearer, but even so, she was aware of an uncomfortable curl of . . . what? Reluctant attraction? Repelled fascination?

The top of her head only came up to his chin, and his size was, paradoxically, both threatening and reassuring. He was large enough to lean on; she was certain if she raised her hand to his chest, he would be solid and warm. Unmovable. Her heart hammered in alarm. He was huge and unwashed, and yet her body reacted to him in the most disconcerting manner.

His stare was uncomfortably intense. She dropped her eyes, breaking the odd frisson between them, and took a small step backward.

His lawn shirt, open at the neck, was so thin it was almost transparent. His muscled chest and arms were clearly visible through the grimy fabric. His breeches were a nondescript brown, snug at the seams, and delineated the hard ridges of muscles of his lean thighs with unnerving clarity.

Georgie frowned. This was a man in the prime of life. It seemed wrong that he'd been caged like an animal. He exuded such a piratical air of command that she could easily imagine him on the prow of a ship or pacing in front of a group of soldiers, snapping orders.

She found her voice. "Were you in the military, Mr. Wylde?"

That would certainly explain his splendid physique and air of cocky confidence.

His dark brows twitched in what might have been surprise but could equally have been irritation. "I was."

She waited for more, but he did not elaborate. Clearly Mr. Wylde was a man of few words. His story was probably like that of thousands of other soldiers who had returned from the wars and found themselves unable to find honest work. She'd seen them in the streets, ragged and begging. It was England's disgrace that men who'd fought so heroically for their country had been reduced to pursuing a life of crime to survive.

Was the fact that he was not a condemned man truly a problem? Her original plan had been to tell Josiah she'd married a sailor who had put to sea. She would have been a widow, of course, but Josiah would never have known that. Her "absent" husband could have sailed the world indefinitely.

If she married this Wylde fellow, she would not immediately become a widow, but the intended result would be the same. Josiah would not be able to force her into marriage and risk committing bigamy.

Georgie narrowed her eyes at the prisoner. They would be bound together until one or the other of them died, and he looked disconcertingly healthy. Providing he didn't take up heavy drinking or catch a nasty tropical disease, he'd probably outlive her. That could cause problems.

Of course, if he continued his ill-advised occupation, then he'd probably succumb to a knife or a bullet sooner rather than later. Men like him always came to a sticky end; he'd only narrowly escaped the gallows this time. She'd probably be a widow in truth soon enough. But how would she hear of his passing if he were halfway across the world? How would she know when she was free?

She tore her eyes away from the rogue's surprisingly tempting lips and fixed Knollys with a hard stare. "Is there really no one else? I mean, he's so...so..."

Words failed her. Intimidating? Manly?

Unmanageable.

"No, ma'am. But he won't bother you after tonight."

What alternative did she have? She couldn't wait another few weeks. Her near-miss with Josiah had been the last straw. She'd been lucky to escape with an awful, sloppy kiss and not complete ruination. She sighed. "He'll have to do. Pieter, will you explain the terms of the agreement?"

Pieter nodded. "You'll marry Miss Caversteed tonight, Mr. Wylde. In exchange, you'll receive five hundred pounds to do with as you will."

Georgie waited for the prisoner to look suitably impressed. He did not. One dark eyebrow rose slightly, and the corner of his mobile lips curled in a most irritating way.

"Fat lot of good it'll do me in here," he drawled. "Ain't got time to pop to a bank between now and when they chain me to that floating death trap in the morning."

He had a fair point. "Is there someone else to whom we could send the money?"

His lips twitched again as if at some private joke. "Aye. Send it to Mr. Wolff at number ten St. James's. The Tricorn Club. Compliments of Ben Wylde. He'll appreciate it."

Georgie had no idea who this Mr. Wolff was—probably someone to whom this wretch owed a gambling debt—but she nodded and beckoned Pieter over. He took his cue and unfolded the legal document she'd had drawn up. He flattened it on the table next to the ordinary's pen and ink.

"You must sign this, Mr. Wylde. Ye can read?" he added as an afterthought.

Another twitch of those lips. "As if I'd been educated at Cambridge, sir. But give me the highlights."

"It says you renounce all claim to the lady's fortune, except for the five hundred pounds already agreed. You will make no further financial demands upon her in the future."

"Sounds reasonable."

The prisoner made a show of studying the entire document, or at least pretending to read it, then dipped the pen into the ink. Georgie held her breath.

Papa's will had divided his property equally between his wife and two daughters. To Georgie's mother, he'd left the estate in Lincolnshire. To her sister, Juliet, he'd left the London town house. And to Georgie, his eldest, the one who'd learned the business at his knee, he'd left the fleet of ships with which he'd made his fortune, the warehouses full of spices and silk, and the company ledgers.

His trusted man of business, Edmund Shaw, had done an exemplary job as Georgie's financial guardian for the past few years, but in three weeks' time, she would turn twenty-five and come into full possession of her fortune. And according to English law, as soon as she married, all that would instantly become the property of her husband, to do with as he wished.

That husband would not be Josiah.

Despite her mother's protests that it was vulgar and unladylike to concern herself with commerce, in the past five years Georgie had purchased two new ships and almost doubled her profits. She loved the challenge of running her own business, the independence. She was damned if she'd give it over to some blithering idiot like Josiah to drink and gamble away.

Which was precisely why she'd had Edmund draw up this detailed document. It stated that all property and capital that was hers before the marriage remained hers. Her husband would receive only a discretionary allowance. To date, she'd received seven offers of marriage, and each time she'd sent her suitor to see Mr. Shaw. Every one of them had balked at signing—proof, if she'd needed it, that they'd only been after her fortune.

She let out a relieved sigh as the prisoner's pen moved confidently over the paper. Ben Wylde's signature was surprisingly neat. Perhaps he'd been a secretary, or written dispatches in the army? She shook her head. It wasn't her job to wonder about him. He was a means to an end, that was all.

He straightened, and his brown eyes were filled with a twinkle of devilry. "There, now. Just one further question, before we get to the vows, Miss Caversteed. Just what do you intend for a wedding night?"

Want to read more? Check out This Earl Of Mine:

ALSO BY KATE BATEMAN

Ruthless Rivals Series:
A Reckless Match
A Daring Pursuit
A Wicked Game

Bow Street Bachelors Series:
This Earl Of Mine
To Catch An Earl
The Princess & The Rogue

Secrets & Spies Series:
To Steal a Heart
A Raven's Heart
A Counterfeit Heart

Italian Renaissance:
The Devil To Pay

Novellas:
The Promise of A Kiss
A Midnight Clear

FOLLOW

Follow Kate online for the latest new releases, giveaways, exclusive sneak peeks, and more!

Follow Kate Online at your favorite retailer

Sign up for Kate's monthly-ish newsletter via her website for news, exclusive excerpts and giveaways.

Join Kate's Facebook reader group: Badasses in Bodices

Follow Kate Bateman on Bookbub for new releases and sales.

Add Kate's books to your Goodreads lists, or leave a review!

ABOUT THE AUTHOR

Kate Bateman / K.C. Bateman, is a bestselling author of Regency and Renaissance historical romances, including the Secrets & Spies series, Bow Street Bachelors series, and Ruthless Rivals series. Her books have received multiple Starred Reviews from Publishers Weekly and Library Journal, and her Renaissance romp The Devil To Pay was a 2019 RITA award nominee.

Her books have been translated into multiple languages, including French, Italian, Brazilian, Japanese, German, Romanian, Czech, and Croatian.

When not writing, Kate leads a double life as a fine art appraiser and on-screen antiques expert for several TV shows in the UK. She currently lives in Illinois with a number-loving husband and three inexhaustible children, and regularly returns to her native England 'for research.'

Kate loves to hear from readers. Contact her via her website: www.kcbateman.com and sign up for her newsletter to receive free books, regular updates on new releases, giveaways, and exclusive excerpts.

Made in the USA
Columbia, SC
17 August 2023

21778389R00079